The Magical
Matchmaker's Legacy

MORNA'S SECRET

USA TODAY BESTSELLING AUTHOR
BETHANY CLAIRE

Editor: J.J. Archer
Cover Designed by Sarah Hansen, Okay Creations

Available In eBook & Paperback

eBook ISBN: 978-0-9978610-8-2
Paperback ISBN: 978-0-9978610-9-9
Hardback ISBN: 978-1-947731-00-4

http://www.bethanyclaire.com

AUTHOR NOTE

AUTHOR NOTE: "Morna's Secret" is the SWEET/CLEAN version of "Love Beyond Reason," originally published in 2013 by Bethany Claire.

CHAPTER 1

J̲ust Outside the Ruins of Conall Castle—Scotland— Present Day

T̲hree days I'd sat in the small room at the inn located only a short distance from the castle ruins. Surrounded by what were now considered artifacts of the castle, I took my time, spending days feigning illness so I could decide what I should do next.

Gwendolyn and Jerry, the kind innkeepers, were growing impatient. I knew they wouldn't allow me to stay in the room much longer without explanation, but what was I to tell them? I could hardly believe the truth myself.

With Adelle's help, and by remaining mostly silent when interacting with them, I'd been able to fool the innkeepers into believing I was Adelle's daughter, Bri. But with Adelle no longer here to speak for me, I knew they would notice my lack of an American accent.

A knock at the door meant it was evening, and Gwendolyn

was bringing my supper. She'd graciously and unquestioningly brought each meal and left it outside the door since I'd arrived back at the inn claiming to be quite ill. She'd given me the privacy I'd desired, and so it surprised me to hear her speak from the other side of the door.

"I'm sorry to disturb your rest, but Jerry and I are both worried about you, dear. You've spent far too much time inside this room, so you've left me no choice, I'm afraid. You can either clean yourself up and join us for dinner downstairs, or I shall be calling a doctor to come see to you."

Gwendolyn paused, waiting for my response. I wasn't ill, only worried, and I wouldn't have them send for a doctor for a non-existent sickness.

"Twill be...I'll be down shortly." A brief response was best. Perhaps my accent wouldn't be as noticeable with only a few quick words. Not that it mattered. I was going to have to tell them all I knew, although I doubted they would believe me.

At this point, I had nothing left to lose.

I walked down the stairs and into the small kitchen to be met by kind smiles from both Gwendolyn and Jerry. The old man gave me a thorough look-over before speaking bluntly, true to form.

"Ye must be feeling much better, lass. Ye doona look sick at all. Now sit down here and tell us where yer mother is. We know something has happened, and it is time that ye tell us what that is. Gwendolyn is too polite to ask ye, but I've no problem with tellin' ye that yer behavior has been quite strange."

The old man stood to usher me to a chair across from both of them. Once I was seated, he resumed his place next to his wife. I sat silently for a moment, quite unsure of where to begin. I knew my accent would garner questions from them right away. "Aye, I'm no longer feeling ill, but I do need to tell ye both something."

Gwendolyn pinched her eyebrows together. "Well, my goodness, Bri. I know it's tempting once you've been here awhile to try and speak like everyone around you, but I've never been very successful at it myself. You sound as if you've lived here forever."

Jerry laughed in response as he patted Gwendolyn on the shoulder. "Aye, my lassie's voice holds nothing of Scotland, although she's lived here for forty years now. She still speaks as if she arrived in the country only yesterday."

Gwendolyn leaned sweetly into Jerry before glancing back at me. "The accent really is great, but why are you doing it?"

I looked down at my plate of untouched food, not quite ready for either of them to think I'd lost my mind.

Jerry reached across the table to gently squeeze my hand and, as I looked up at him, I could see the concern in his face. "Where's yer mother, lass?"

"She's not my mother. And I'm not Bri. I doona think ye will believe what I must tell ye, but will ye listen to all of it before ye decide that I'm mad?" I lifted my head to look them in the eyes as I waited for their answer.

Jerry and Gwendolyn exchanged an unreadable sideways glance before Jerry spoke first. "Aye, lass. O'course we shall listen to ye. Let us move next to the fire, though. The chairs in there are much more comfortable."

Gwendolyn simply nodded before they both stood and led me into the next room.

Once seated, I fumbled uneasily with my words, unsure of how to begin. One question had sat at the forefront of my mind since the first night I'd left Adelle at the castle ruins. I'd been too afraid to ask, for if the answer was not what I hoped, it meant everyone I'd known and loved had died only days ago, unable to change history. I knew that I must learn the truth before I explained anything further to Jerry and Gwendolyn.

"Might I ask ye a question first?" I dinna wait for their response. "The castle ruins, I suppose they're still ruins, aye?"

Hope fluttered in my chest at their quizzical expressions.

Jerry pointed in the direction of the castle. "Do ye mean Conall Castle, lass? If so, I wouldna go calling the place a ruin. It's still beautifully intact—a fine structure and a popular visit for tourists."

I was unsure of what a "tourist" was, but if what he said was true, it meant that they'd been successful at stopping the attack. Adelle, Bri, Eoin, Mary, and Arran had most likely all gone on to live for many more years. That knowledge was enough to rid me of any other fears I had about moving on alone in this time.

"Do ye really mean it? The castle is not just a pile of rocks? It wasna destroyed long ago?" I needed just one more reassurance in order to fully believe him.

Gwendolyn nodded. "Yes, dear. The Conalls have been one of the most powerful and beloved clans in Scotland for centuries. Descendants still own the castle, but they've partnered with the historical society to open it up for visitors. Are you sure you're not ill?"

I nodded, relieved beyond explanation. It was time to tell them what had happened. Then, regardless of their reaction, it was time for me to move on from this place and start a new life on my own.

"Aye, I feel fine. But I need to tell ye what's happened, and 'tis a long story." I sighed. "I doubt ye will believe me."

Jerry smiled and sat back in his chair, settling in. "Why doona ye just get on with it, lass? Then we will decide what to believe."

"Aye. I'm not sure of where to begin. The first thing I should tell ye is that I'm not Bri. My name is Blaire MacChristy. My father was laird of MacChristy Castle during the seventeenth century. I was betrothed to Alasdair Conall's eldest son, Eoin. But on the day of our wedding in the year sixteen hundred and forty-five, I found myself swept up by a spell cast by Alasdair's late sister, Morna Conall, a witch who died when I was very young. As you can see, Bri and I look verra much the same with our hair dark and our eyes blue, and Morna knew that we would. She cast the spell so that if Bri and I ever laid eyes on the same spelled plaque in a room beneath the castle, we would switch places in time. Nearly two months ago, her spell worked. Bri was sent back, and I was brought forward." I paused to look up at them and was stunned that they both seemed rather unsurprised by my words.

"Lass, why did Morna want ye to switch places?" asked Jerry, as if we were having the most normal of conversations. "And where is Adelle?"

Was it possible that he believed me? It took me a moment to find my voice. "That's why I asked ye if the castle was in ruins. When I arrived here, it was. When Adelle and Bri came here, it was, as well. According to Adelle's research, only a few short months after my wedding, the Conalls were murdered and the castle destroyed. No one ever found out who murdered them, and that was why Bri and Adelle came to Scotland—to search for something that might reveal who had murdered the Conalls. 'Tis the same reason that Morna cast the spell. She hoped that if Bri and I switched places, Bri's knowledge of what was to come would enable her to stop the attack, or at least change the outcome of it. And she did. If not, then the castle would still be in ruins now."

"And Adelle?" Jerry continued to stare at me as if he wasn't shocked by my story.

"Once Adelle realized that we'd been switched, we spent weeks searching for a spell that could switch us back. We found one, but Bri dinna want to return. She married Eoin in my place, and they fell in love after the wedding. I dinna want to go back either. There's not much left for me there." I paused as an uncomfortable knot lodged itself in my chest. Swallowing hard, I continued, "Adelle wanted to be with Bri. So she did the spell instead, and it worked. She's with Bri now. 'Twas three days ago when I arrived here alone telling ye I was sick. I dinna know what to do." I leaned back in my chair and crossed my hands in my lap.

Gwendolyn remained silent, and I could tell nothing by her expression.

The three of us sat in silence for what seemed like an eternity. Eventually, Gwendolyn stood and walked to the other side of the room. Reaching up to the top of the bookshelf lining the wall, she pulled a small box from the shelf.

She returned to her seat next to Jerry and smiled at him quickly before extending the box in my direction. "I'd like to tell you a story myself if you don't mind, dear."

Confused, I only nodded and took the box, placing it in my lap.

Gwendolyn pointed at the box. "Open it, and pull out the photographs."

I lifted the small metal latch that kept the lid closed and looked down inside the box. I remembered the first time I'd seen a photograph on the first day I'd arrived in this time. Adelle had shown me one of Bri to emphasize just how much we resembled one another. Despite all the strange and wonderful things I'd seen, it was still miraculous to me that moments could be captured forever on a small piece of parchment.

Only three photographs lay inside, all facing down, and I lifted them out and closed the lid before turning them over. As I gazed at the images, the air around me chilled suddenly.

The first was of Conall Castle, but not as I remembered it. It was the castle in ruins as it had been when I arrived in this time.

The second was of the spelled plaque, still painted with my portrait. A reminder of the day my life had changed forever.

The first two images were shocking, but it was the third that caused my hands to shake and my breath to come out unsteadily as I glanced up at Gwendolyn. She only smiled softly, waiting for me to speak.

The third photograph was less a picture and more of a painted portrait, depicting people I'd known in my old life. Alasdair, young and vibrant, holding a baby Arran in his arms, while Eoin, no more than five and only knee-high, stood next to his father. Alasdair's other arm was draped around a woman's shoulder, squeezing her tightly with affection. The woman was not Alasdair's late wife, who had died giving birth to Arran, and I knew there was only one other person the woman could be. She was the witch, Morna.

While her face in the portrait was younger, it matched Gwendolyn's exactly.

*G*wendolyn eventually gave up on waiting for me to respond. Laughing heartily, she reached out and squeezed my hand. "Come, dear. Surely after all you've been through, nothing can be too much of a surprise to you."

I looked over at Jerry, and he nodded in confirmation.

I gasped. "Do ye mean? How could ye be her?" I asked Gwendolyn. "Morna died when I was a verra small child."

"There are a far manner of things, dear, that seem impossible. Surely this is no more impossible than you sitting here in this century when you were born in another, aye?"

Gwendolyn slowly lost the American accent she'd been using the entire time I'd known her. She was right. After all I'd been through, I had no trouble believing her, but I didn't understand how or why she was here.

"If ye could end up here after yer own death, then why would ye bother with the spell for me and Bri?" I asked. "Could ye not have stopped the massacre yerself?"

Gwendolyn, or Morna, I wan't sure which name was now appropriate, smiled as if she had expected my question.

"Because, lass, there are more important things than life and death. My spell put into motion other things just as important as saving the lives of my family members. Souls needed to meet. Souls that belonged together, despite being born centuries apart. Without my spell, that could never have been."

"Do ye mean Eoin and Bri?" Looking at her more closely, I noticed for the first time her resemblance to Alasdair, Eoin, and Arran. The shape of their eyes, the slant of their smiles, all strong Conall traits that made me trust her story even more.

"Aye. Eoin and Bri. Not to mention, there was my own lad, who dinna exist in my own time. Instead of saving my family myself, I chose to sit back and watch over those who would save them, while at the same time finding the man I was meant to love."

"Ye mean, Jerry isna like ye?" I asked.

Jerry cackled and coughed before he spoke. "No, lassie! I was born right here, in this time. And if I had the gift of magic like my wife, I'd have stopped my knees from cracking long ago."

Morna frowned at her husband. "I've told ye before, I could stop it for ye myself, but ye willna let me." She turned toward me once more. "He accepts the truth, but it all still makes him a wee bit uncomfortable. He willna let me use magic on him."

"So ye mean ye knew I wasna Bri?"

"Aye, lass. But I'll tell ye, I dinna expect ye to stay here and Adelle to go back. My visions dinna show me that. Perhaps they dinna want me to try and stop it from happening. Are ye certain that ye wish to stay here?"

Panic shot through me at the thought of going back. "Aye! I canna go back." I answered too quickly, startling both Morna and Jerry.

Morna's face softened, her eyes showing that she understood. "All right, lass. Well, what is it that ye want to do now? We shall help ye get settled wherever ye'd like to go. Do ye wish to stay in Scotland?"

I'd given it no thought. I'd been too concerned with what I was going to tell them, and whether or not Adelle and Bri had been able to stop the massacre, to think much further than a few moments into my future. "I'm not sure. I doona know what to do."

Jerry leaned over and squeezed my hand, and there was no doubt in my mind that Morna had chosen well. Her husband was the best of men—kind to his core.

Morna waved a hand in the air, as if dismissing my concern. "Doona worry. Why doona we help ye get settled in Edinburgh? We could get ye a job and a place to stay, and ye can see how ye like it for a while. If ye decide later that ye'd like to go elsewhere, then we'll be more than happy to help ye."

"Aye, that will be fine. Thank ye. I suppose ye shall be glad to have another empty room for guests, aye?"

Morna stood and motioned for me to do the same, and then we made our way to the stairs. Clearly, we were all about to retire for the evening.

"Lass, we doona allow other guests. Ye are the only one who knows this house is here. Only yerself and those I wish to see it can see this house along the side of the road. We'd be overrun with tourists, otherwise."

CHAPTER 2

onall Castle – Scotland – 1646

*A*rran Conall made his way down to the stables for his daily ride. The remaining men of what was formerly the Kinnaird Clan still camped out on the castle grounds nearly two months after the demise of the clan's wretched laird.

Laird Kinnaird had given birth to no sons, and with his daughter still unmarried, the clan remained at Conall Castle under Eoin's blessing while they tried to sort out a way to name their next leader.

Arran found himself stifled while standing in an open field. With guests tucked into every free corner of the castle and its grounds, his daily rides and work in the stables were all that kept him from insanity.

He needed to keep busy, anyway. The loss of his beloved Blaire to a century beyond his comprehension occupied his thoughts every moment. He was happy that his brother had found love in his new wife, Bri, but with her face so similar to

Blaire's, Arran was reminded of his own heartache every time he laid eyes on his new sister-in-law.

If he'd known his rejection of Blaire would send her so far from him, he would have defied his brother and never let her go. He would live with the regret of hurting her for the rest of his life.

Arran shook his head, doing his best to dislodge all thoughts of his beloved from his conscious mind. He saw enough of Blaire in his dreams. It was torture to see her in the recesses of his mind when he was awake, as well.

Rounding the corner of the entrance to the stables, he found Edana Kinnaird, the daughter of the late, villainous laird, feeding an apple to his brother's old horse, Griffin. The stables were usually occupied by only the castle's fleet of horses and the old stable master, Kip. But Arran was surprised to find that his spirits lifted at the sight of his new friend.

While many women and children of Kinnaird's clan had stayed inside the castle, Edana was the only one who had her own room upstairs, where members of the Conall family resided. For the past months, Edana had stayed in Arran's late mother's room, just down the hall from his own. He saw her often, and although she always kept their conversations short, he could tell by the way she watched him that she fancied him.

He could never return her feelings. His own heart had been swept away to a different time with another lass. If he'd met Edana only a year ago, he'd have already broken her heart without as much as a second thought. But Blaire had changed him irreparably, and it caused him to look at Edana's feelings toward him in a kinder light. He liked the lass, and he respected her. He wanted to do all he could to show her friendship.

She'd been through much as a child, living with her brute of a father. Arran was certain Kinnaird had abused the young girl physically, and maybe in even more unthinkable ways, as well.

She seemed a kindhearted lass, and with all her family gone, Arran knew she must be terrified over the uncertainty of her future.

Smiling wide, he made his way toward her, reaching up to rub Griffin behind his ears as he stopped beside the horse.

"Ah, Griffin. Ye are a lucky lad today. I'm sure ye are glad to be receiving such a treat from a lady rather than from me or Kip, aye?" Arran turned and winked at Edana. "Ye shall spoil him, lass. I fear he shall never take an apple from me again. He'll always want to eat it out of yer delicate hands."

Edana blushed, and Arran didn't miss how she averted her eyes from him before speaking.

"Nay, I doubt it. He doesna seem too particular about who's giving him the apple. He only wants to eat it."

"I doona know about that. I canna think of a time I've seen him look so pleased." Arran continued to stroke Griffin, hoping that if he looked distracted with the horse, it would ease Edana's nerves. "What are ye doing down here? I doona believe I've seen ye in the stables before."

"I'm grateful that ye and yer brother have allowed me to stay here. Lady Bri is exceedingly kind, but I tire of being indoors, and I canna stand to hear the men speak any further about how they shall replace me father." Edana's brow creased in a pained expression.

Arran reached forward to place a hand on her shoulder to comfort her. She jerked away from him as if touched by fire, and Arran quickly went back to stroking Griffin. "I doona blame ye for needing to get away, but doona be worried about yer clan, lass. No matter who takes over as laird, ye shall not lose yer place in the castle. I promise that I'll see that ye are provided for just as ye have always been."

Edana fumbled with her hands nervously, obviously unsure of how to respond. Arran didn't press her. As he turned and began to walk away to see to the other horses, she called out to him. "Thank ye, Arran. I doona deserve yer kindness. I'm not as good as ye think I am."

Arran stopped walking and spun to face Edana. "Doona talk in that manner, lass. Ye deserve every kindness in the world." He paused, deciding that he could attend to the stables later. Perhaps what the lass needed most was to be left alone. "Now, I'll leave ye in peace. Spend as much time with the horses as ye wish. If ye decide ye would like to go for a ride, Kip would be more than happy to assist ye."

Smiling briefly, he turned and left. Perhaps it was time he talked to his brother about their guests. The Kinnaird clan needed to choose a new leader and return to their own castle and territory. He didn't like to see Edana so distressed. The least he could do for her was to see her safely settled.

---

*E*dana Kinnaird watched until she was sure Arran was out of sight. Shivering beneath her clothes, she reached up to brush her shoulder harshly where he'd touched her. She could scrub the spot all day and it would never be enough to rid her of the Conall filth that he'd placed there.

She couldn't stand another moment in captivity here. Each day she spent with the ever-kind and polite Conalls made her hate them that much more.

Her father had been a horrible man. Violent, angry, and disgusting, he'd beaten her mother's spirit until she'd died of sadness. He'd spent much of his life trying to do the same to Edana. But she was far stronger than her mother. Her father had even admitted that much.

Edana had always hated her father, but he was all she'd had in the world, and she would never be able to forgive the family responsible for his death. She had even gone to the Conalls before her father's planned attack, warning them that he planned to murder them. She'd been confused, torn between misplaced loyalty to a father who hated her, and an unbidden wish to see him fail because she hated him, too. And that confusion had caused her not to think straight. It didn't occur to her then that trying to do the right thing would cost her everything.

Despite Arran's well-intentioned promises, she knew now that as soon as a leader rose up among the cowardly men of her father's clan, she would lose her place as lady of the keep. The new laird would marry, and Edana would be cast out, hated for her father's crimes.

Edana was through helplessly waiting to see what would take place. She'd learned enough of manipulation from her father to know that she had Arran just where she wanted him. With each quick glance away from him and each blush of her cheeks, she knew he grew to believe she cared for him. That belief would make him weak, as love does to all people, and then she would be in the perfect position to save her legacy for herself.

With each bat of her lashes in Arran's direction, the desperate seed of revenge took root, twisting its way through every last corner of her mind as she worked out a way to continue her father's work and destroy the Conalls.

She'd failed her father once by giving away his plan. She would not disappoint him again.

CHAPTER 3

"*J*ust stay still for a minute, Mom. Can't you tell I'm trying to talk to you about something?" Bri reached to grab the side of her mother's dress, hoping it would deter Adelle from continuing the raid on her closet—a habit her mother had developed in the twenty-first century. Now, Bri only owned a handful of dresses, yet her mother still enjoyed stealing her clothes.

"Do you think I could talk Mary into making a few more gowns for me?" her mom asked. "She does such lovely work."

Adelle turned and joined Bri at the end of the bed. Quickly hiking up her dress, she kicked off her shoes and jumped up onto the feathered ticking so that she sat cross-legged, facing Bri. Both women, while now considered beloved members of the family, stood out as oddities in this century. Their relaxed social manners and American accents branded them as the foreigners they were.

Bri smiled, amazed at her mother's vanity when they now lived in a place where mirrors were few and far between. The mere fact that they had all their teeth set them apart as rare beauties here. "I'm sure Mary would be happy to sew for you, Mom, but I expect she will have you chipping in on a lot of the work."

Adelle laughed. "Oh yes, I expect that she will. Now, what is it that you were wanting to talk about?"

"Blaire." Bri paused, knowing that the mention of her lookalike would cause a reaction from her mother.

"Oh. Why?" Adelle sighed. "I miss the sweet girl terribly, but there's nothing I can do for her here except hope and pray that she's happy and has adjusted well." Her eyes shifted downward, an odd occurrence for such a forthright woman and a sure sign she truly was heartsick over the idea of Blaire being left in the twenty-first century all alone.

"Well, maybe there is something we can do. I've been spending a lot of time in the spell room—"

"What? Bri, you have no business ever entering that room again. It's already taken you from me once," Adelle exclaimed, interrupting Bri, her voice shrill and panicked. "Besides, I like it here. I don't want to have to follow you if you're sucked back through time again."

Bri rolled her eyes at the expected melodramatics. "It isn't some big wormhole with a magnetic pull that's going to suck me in. It's all based on Morna's spells, Mom. And there are others that can work, that could bring us back and forth as we please. I'm sure there are risks, but I think they might be worth taking."

"What for? I didn't keep Blaire from returning here, Bri. She suggested that I go in her place. She didn't want to come back. She chose to stay."

Bri nodded. "I know all that, but *why* did she not want to come back? Did she ever tell you?" When Adelle shook her head, Bri added, "I think she was heartbroken."

Adelle's face blanched and her eyes widened with surprise.

"She never spoke of it, but I think you might be right. She said that there was no longer anything here for her, as if she had lost something dear."

"Have you noticed the way Arran avoids me at almost all cost? When we do run into each other, the look in his eyes breaks my heart." Bri sighed, and at the sight of her mother's confused expression, continued, "I guess I never told you about what happened with Arran, did I?" Bri smiled as she watched the color return to her mother's face with the anticipation of a juicy story.

"No, I've never noticed. And no, you never told me! But, I expect you to right this instant," Adelle said, her eyes lighting up.

Bri adjusted herself on the edge of the bed, reaching for a cushion to prop herself up more comfortably, knowing she was prolonging her mother's impatience. "The night of my wedding to Eoin, Arran came to our bedchamber door thinking it was his own. He was very drunk. Anyway, Eoin was helping put out a small fire at the reception, so I had to help Arran down to his own room. To make a long story short, he kissed me. Granted, he thought I was Blaire, but it was clear that the two of them had been involved. And that he loves her very much."

"Oh, wow. So you're telling me that you've kissed both of them?" Adelle paused and waved her hand in the air in dismissal. "Never mind, that's beside the point. But you know, I do remember that Arran seemed upset the day I arrived and told you that Blaire chose to stay."

"Yes, he was, and I'm worried about him. Each day he drinks a little more than he did the day before. He's broken. I want to go and talk to Blaire, let her know that Arran is still in love with her and see if she would want to come back. Do you think that she would, Mom?" Bri sat patiently while her mother thought about the question. Finally, Adelle looked up and into Bri's eyes.

"I don't know, honey. She was very private. The two of you

may look alike, but you are quite different. She was curious about modern things and did her best to keep our conversations on that topic. She didn't ever want to talk about herself."

Bri shifted uncomfortably, her resolve regarding her decision to meddle in Arran's affairs shaky. "There is another reason why I'd like to go back—some unfinished business that I feel I should take care of."

Adelle's eyebrows rose, nearly reaching the top of her hairline. "What's that, dear?"

"Several things, actually. School, Mitsy, and putting an end to the missing persons report I'm certain Mitsy has filed. I need to clear things up with her and stop any police department searches for me that might be underway."

Adelle shook her head. "Nobody's searching. While Blaire and I were at the inn, the police called looking for you. I instructed Gwendolyn and Jerry to tell them you were fine but did not wish to speak to them. I called the station back later pretending to be you so they'd close the missing persons report. I also falsified reports from the dig and scheduled them to be sent out at different intervals for the next three months. Most likely, the grant committee is just now starting to realize that something is off."

"Well, that's good to know. I'm glad my disappearance didn't make national news."

Mom studied me for a few minutes, then asked, "Are you sure you want to do this? Eoin will never let you go."

"Eoin isn't going to keep me from going anywhere. I'm sure he will be against it, but it's something I must do. Arran needs Blaire, and Mitsy needs to know what happened to me. It's only weeks until her wedding. I won't have her ruin her big day by worrying over me."

Adelle stood, and Bri remained on the bed as her mother

made her way to the bedchamber door. "I know you will do what you feel is right. Good luck telling this to Eoin. You are far braver than I."

---

*A*ustin, TX – Present Day

*M*itsy soon-to-be Fredrickson stood across the desk from Principal Hendricks, the twin of Mr. Clean. With her arms crossed firmly across her chest, she tapped her foot.

"Look. I didn't come here to ask your permission, Principal Hendricks. I've already booked the flight. You can either approve the days, or I'll quit. But either way, I'm going to Scotland to look for Bri. I'm only asking to leave a week earlier than I was originally scheduled to be off for my wedding, anyway. The substitute has been here for months now. She doesn't need me in the classroom with her. Now, are you going to sign off on it, or do I need to submit my resignation?"

Principal Hendricks crossed his own arms and looked her up and down as if gauging the seriousness of her words. "You know that the police have already closed the case, Mitsy, and we've already terminated Ms. Montgomery's contract here with the district. The police chief told you himself that they have confirmation in Scotland that Bri is unharmed and still in the country. Ms. Montgomery did this to herself. Why do you feel the need to seek her out?"

Mitsy's head pounded as her blood pressure rose. When she spoke, her voice came out harsher than intended, but she couldn't rein in her frustration. "Some old innkeeper telling the police that the girl they've described is staying with them is not confirmation that she's all right. Neither is them speaking to someone who is supposedly Bri on the phone. The innkeepers said she wouldn't take my calls. Bri wouldn't refuse to talk to me. She knows me, and she knows how worried I'd be. Don't you understand my concern? The couple the police talked to could have murdered her!" Mitsy sat down in the chair opposite Principal Hendricks, her legs shaky and unsteady.

"The police also contacted the archaeological society that Bri's mother worked for. They said that they've received reports on the dig regularly, the last one arriving only a week ago. Bri accompanied her mother on the dig."

Mitsy reached up and tucked a fistful of springy red curls behind her ears, the principal's words doing nothing to calm her down. "I know. I know all of this, but something has gone wrong. Bri is the least impulsive person I've ever known. She lives every day by a strict schedule, and she's my best friend. She would not abandon me without good reason, and she wouldn't miss the wedding. She knows I'd kill her myself."

As Principal Hendricks drummed his fingertips on the top of his desk, Mitsy had to grab onto both of her elbows to keep from slamming her palms down hard on top of his hand. She fidgeted impatiently as she waited for him to respond.

"I'm not going to change your mind, am I?" she asked when she couldn't stand to wait another second.

"You know the days off aren't the issue. I'm just worried about you, is all. As a friend, not as your principal. I don't think you are going to be happy with what you find in Scotland. I truly believe that Bri just decided to abandon her life here. It's best that you move on and forget about her. Try and enjoy the wedding and this new phase of your life."

Mitsy knew he was wrong. Every fiber of her being screamed

it. She stood and made her way to the door, pausing there to turn back toward him briefly. "So the days are approved? Great. I'll see you at the wedding."

Slamming the door of his office behind her, she made her way home to pack for her flight.

CHAPTER 4

S cotland – 1646

"*Y* e canna mean it, Bri!" Eoin's eyes flared, relaying his grave concern. "Morna's spells are unpredictable. Father told me countless stories of how they often went awry, causing havoc around the castle. Ye canna be sure that all will proceed to your liking, love."

Bri hesitated before speaking, knowing that she needed to be careful of how she approached this conversation with Eoin. She was going to do the spell regardless of his liking; she'd already made up her mind. But already in her few short months of marriage, she'd learned that if she wanted to get what she wanted, it was best to make her husband feel as if he had come up with the idea himself.

"The spell has worked correctly several times, has it not? You were even prepared to send me back using it when the Kinnaird clan planned to attack us. Surely you wouldn't have done so if you weren't certain all would go smoothly, right?" Bri placed a hand on his broad shoulder, snuggling in close to weaken his resolve.

She smiled as Eoin buried his face in her hair, kissing the top of her head. "Aye, love. I did believe that the spell would work, but I'm so verra glad that ye dinna do it. By the time she died, Morna was a great caster."

Bri breathed in the heady scent of her husband before shaking her head to bring herself back to task. "So, you see? It would be safe for me to go. You've basically just said so yourself."

A squeal escaped Bri's lips as Eoin trailed kisses along the side of her neck, then nipped her earlobe gently between his teeth.

"Ye are twisting my words, lass," he murmured, his deep voice scattering goosebumps over her skin. "While I do believe the spells willna cause ye harm, that doesna mean I think ye should go. Are ye so sure that Arran feels the way that ye say? I've not heard him speak of Blaire."

Bri stepped back so she could look into Eoin's face. Just the sight of his ebony eyes and hair took her breath away. Smiling, she continued, "Do you not remember the night of our wedding?"

"Ye think I could forget, love?"

Eoin's smile warmed her from the inside out. "Arran may have been drunk, but he wouldn't have kissed me so if he didn't feel there was a reason to," she said. "He and Blaire had kissed before. I believe they were in love."

Bri repressed a laugh as she watched Eoin's eyebrows draw together and his lips twist in muddled confusion. "Nay! Are ye telling me that my own betrothed and my arse of a brother were together before the wedding? I should tear the lousy sot to bits."

"Oh, hush. It's not as if you loved Blaire. From what I've gathered, you couldn't stand her, so what does it matter if Arran could? It's very difficult to control who you fall in love with, Eoin. Besides, if things hadn't happened as they had, it's very possible I wouldn't have ended up here. Surely you wouldn't have wanted that?"

Air quickly escaped Bri's lungs as Eoin crushed her against him, pressing his mouth to hers in a desperate kiss, leaving them both breathless. "Nay, lass, I wouldna want that. I canna stand the thought of ye not being by my side. So, I must ask one thing of ye, if ye are to do this."

Bri stepped away from him, her insides weak and fluttery from his kiss, her curiosity piqued. "What is it?"

"I shall come with ye. If the spell goes wrong, and ye are trapped in another time, I will be with ye."

"You can't be serious, Eoin. For starters, we have no modern male clothes to put you in. I, at least, still have the clothes I was wearing when I arrived here. You would stand out like a sore thumb!"

"A sore thumb, lass?"

Bri couldn't help but laugh aloud at the look of confusion flickering across Eoin's face. "Forget it. But that's another reason why you can't possibly come. You wouldn't be able to communicate. Not to mention how confused you will be by cars, cell phones, ATMs."

Eoin placed his hands on her shoulders. "Aye, lass. It doesna sound so different from the way ye were when ye first arrived here. And ye survived. I shall have ye to help me, and I find myself curious to see the world belonging to my strange, bonny lass."

He smiled sweetly, and Bri found herself softening to the idea. It would be nice not to be all alone. And she agreed with him; if something did go wrong with the spell, she couldn't stand the thought of being separated from him. Besides, watching his reaction to the conveniences of modern times was sure to be a humorous and fascinating experience. Now that he'd presented the idea, she found herself eager to take him up on it.

"Fine. But on one condition," she said.

"Anything."

"While we are there, I am the boss. Life is very different in my world. For your own safety, you need to do whatever I tell you to do. Understood?"

Eoin rolled his eyes, and Bri smiled, anticipating what he was going to say even before he spoke.

"Aye, lass. As if ye are not my master already. It shall be little adjustment from daily life now."

"That's right." Bri winked playfully. "And don't you forget it, mister. Now you'll need to think of something to tell Arran. He will have to know we are going somewhere, but it's best he doesn't know the truth. He would try to stop us from going."

"Aye, he would. I shall talk to him now."

*A*rran made his way through the castle's winding hallways, stopping to briefly poke his head in the kitchen to pester the beloved housemaid, cook, and mentor, Mary. He stepped inside the long room and sneakily stuck his hand out to grab at one of the loaves of bread set aside for the evening meal.

He was rewarded with the expected quick smack on his hand.

"How many times do I have to tell ye? Ye are not going to get food from this kitchen until 'tis served to ye, as long as I am here. And doona get yer hopes up, I intend to live many more decades still."

Arran laughed and bent to scoop Mary up in a large embrace, roughly kissing her on the cheek. "Aye, I surely hope that ye do. The castle would fall apart without ye, Mary." He continued to squeeze her, her feet dangling inches off the ground, refusing to set her down until she screeched and reached over his shoulder to swat at something behind him.

He quickly set the plump woman back on the floor and spun to see what had her in such a fuss. Eoin stood with his hand extended toward the bread, guilt spread across his face.

Mary waved Eoin away from the aromatic loaves. "Ye shall drive me mad! The both of ye. It doesna matter how many times I repeat myself, ye doona seem to hear it. Now get." She paused and extended both of her arms out in front of her, palms up, and briskly shooed them from the kitchen. "I doona want to see yer faces until the evening meal. Get on with ye."

"Aye."

"Aye."

Their voices echoed as, in unison, they each kissed Mary on the cheek and quickly made their leave of her place of worship. Once outside, Arran faced Eoin.

Once outside, Arran walked alongside Eoin. "I've been looking for ye, brother. I need to speak with ye about the visiting clan. It's been months, and they've still made no decision regarding a new leader. We canna allow them to stay here forever."

"Aye, ye are right. But that shall have to wait for a few days."

Arran paused, turning to lean against the wall so that his brother would do the same. "Has something happened?"

Eoin shook his head, and Arran instantly felt relieved. He didn't think he could bear any more tragedies so soon after the death of his father and the loss of his beloved.

"Nay, but Bran – from the village – ye remember him, aye?"

Arran nodded. "Aye, o'course. What of him?"

"He has asked that I come to help him with the building of a stable. He canna afford to pay anyone to help. He knew, as his friend, I would. Bri shall go along with me and help his wife with their brood of children."

Arran was certain Bran already had a stable, but he decided not to question his brother's story. With Eoin gone, perhaps he'd have ample time to resolve the situation with their guests on his own.

"Aye, 'tis kind of ye to agree to help him. Do ye need me to go along, as well?" Arran hoped Eoin would say no, but it was formality that he should offer assistance.

"Nay. I need ye to stay here and serve as laird while I'm gone," Eoin responded. "I shan't be far, but I doona want ye to try and find me with castle issues. I trust ye to see to anything that may arise while I am gone."

"O'course. Wish Bran and his family well for me. When will ye be leaving?"

"Tomorrow, I believe. I shall leave ye now. I left my wife in our bedchamber all alone. I am anxious to return to her."

Arran smiled and waved his brother off. "Aye, I'm sure ye are."

Once Eoin left, Arran slowly made his way back to his own bedchamber. While his brother was away, he would focus his time and attention on finding a solution to their guests' dilemma regarding a new leader. And he would focus on solving Edana's problem, as well. If he succeeded, he knew his brother would be pleased.

At the very least, Eoin would be happy to have things around the castle resume a more normal pace. And Arran knew it would be good for him to have something else to focus his mind upon other than Blaire. He might not love Edana, but he could make sure that she was taken care of. Aye, as far as he was concerned, his brother's trip to the village could not have come at a better time.

CHAPTER 5

*E*dinburgh, Scotland – Present Day

I was certain I'd never heard such language from a lady. I did my best to listen to the angry woman, but with each breath Danny's voice grew louder, and I found my mind drifting away from the conversation. Not that I was given much chance to speak. The old lady—my boss—waved her finger at me in such a manner I was certain it would fall off.

A momentary second of silence caused me to refocus my attention.

"'Ello? Are ye daft in the head, Blaire? Have ye been listening to a word I've said?" Danny threw her hands violently up in the air only to bring them down swiftly so they sat snugly on her hips. She glared at me, unblinking.

"Aye. I did hear ye, but I doona understand. There's no reason why the two of them should have been asleep so late in the day. They werena sick, and 'tis dreadful behavior." I knew my words would be met with more screaming, and I felt the tips of my ears pull back, readying for the inevitable attack.

"Ye are a bloody fool! If only I had the luxury of sleeping in one day in my lousy life, I would take full advantage. It is not yer place to decide how long our paying guests sleep in the morning. I've told ye before, if they are in the room, skip it and go on to the next room for cleaning. Come back to it later, after they wake and leave for the day."

"Aye, I willna do it again." I turned to leave, hoping that if I slipped away fast enough the lecture would be over. But I only took one step before Danny grabbed my arm.

"Ye turn back around. I dinna dismiss ye. Ye are right, ye willna do it again because ye are no longer employed by this hotel."

Danny looked at me, satisfaction evident on her face, but as I continued to adjust to the many unfamiliar words of this time, I dinna understand what she was telling me. "I'm sorry. I doona understand ye. No longer employed?"

"Fired. Doona show up for work here again. I doona want to see ye around here. If this was yer first transgression, then ye would only be getting a warning, but there have been many complaints."

Twas cold, but sweat beaded on my forehead as understanding settled in. I no longer had a job. "Complaints?"

"Aye, lass. Complaints. Many. More than one family said they saw ye sweeping the carpet rather than using the vacuum. Another said they saw ye hanging the sheets up in the room to be beaten with the broom handle. Who taught ye to clean? Yer great-great-great grandmother?" Danny laughed slightly, pleased with herself for the odd joke.

"No one taught me to clean. I doona like the sound of the vacuum; it hurts my ears. And I doona know how to use the cleaning barrel for the sheets."

Danny's eyes grew wide at my ignorance.

"Cleaning barrel? Do ye mean the washing machine? Gracious! I'd hate to see what yer house looks like, and I bet yer clothes smell something dreadful. Now, collect yer things and be gone with ye."

She gave me no further chance to speak as she turned and left, leaving me alone in the small storage room beneath the staircase. I knew I'd been in trouble when she pulled me into the broom storage, but I never expected to be left without a job.

Without it, I had little means to pay for the small apartment Jerry and Morna had found for me, and I was unsure of how to search for another job. What could I do? I had few skills, and those I did possess would serve me little in today's time.

I'd held the job for only two weeks. With each passing day, I found myself regretting my decision to stay in this time just a little bit more.

But it didn't matter. I alone had chosen my path. Breathing in deeply, I tried to suck back the tears threatening to fall from my eyes. I lifted my head up and left the closet.

"*W*ait up!" I heard the shout from behind me but continued to make my way home, assuming the words were meant for someone else.

"Blaire! Slow down. Ye walk so fast I canna catch up with ye."

I stopped walking, causing a man who seemed to be in quite a big hurry to walk right into my back. After he told me what he thought about me in a few short, fairly shocking words, I turned to see one of the other maids, Isla, lifting her dainty, short legs up in an effort to reach me.

"I'm sorry," I said. "I thought ye were calling after someone else."

Once Isla was next to me, we moved off of the main walkway so we could stand without blocking the way of others. Isla rubbed her gloved hands together and cupped them around her mouth, blowing air into them to warm them.

I continued to be amazed at how cold everyone here seemed to always be. 'Twas no colder than Scotland always was. With the thick coats and protective clothing that people now wore, not to mention my favorite modern invention—heaters, I found the temperature to always be quite pleasant.

"No, I was talking to you," Isla told me. "I just got off work, and I heard about what Danny did. I'm sorry about yer job, but ye did do things awful strange. But what I wanted to say is, I might could get ye another job, if ye like."

"Aye, I would like. I doona know what I will do, otherwise."

Isla smiled and put her arm around me as if we were much more closely acquainted. "I thought that might be the case. There is a catch, though. Ye canna do this job looking like ye do. It would only cause trouble for ye."

I stepped away, still uncomfortable with the familiarity people of this time used with one another. "What do ye mean? What is the job?"

"My cousin owns a pub not far from the hotel. I've been bartending there as a second job, but I canna juggle both at the same time. He's looking for a replacement for me. I would train ye myself, and I know he will give ye the job if I ask him. All ye do is mix drinks, but ye look too pretty and sweet with yer long hair and clean face. I know ye have enough spunk to handle the job, but yer appearance needs to reflect yer no-nonsense attitude. I'll help ye change yer look. What do ye say?" Isla smiled and shrugged her shoulders, raising her hands, palms up, as if awaiting my answer.

I knew it would be foolish to tell her no. "Aye, I canna thank ye enough, Isla. What do ye want to do about my appearance?"

I fidgeted uncomfortably while Isla looked me up and down, deciding how to best alter what was apparently so unacceptable about me. "How would ye feel about cutting yer hair? And maybe piercing yer ears? And eyeliner, ye definitely need to learn how to employ the use of eyeliner. It will make ye look more intimidating instantly. Believe me, when tending bar for a bunch of rowdy Scots, ye want a look that says 'doona even think about it.'"

"Aye, if ye say so. But I doona wanna look like a man. The hair goes no higher than my shoulders." I reached a hand up to run through my long locks. Mayhap a change would be good.

"Deal."

With that, Isla led me in another direction, away from my new home. We walked for what seemed like miles. My feet felt heavy and tired from working all day at the hotel. At last, Isla turned us onto a dimly lit street where we made our way into what she called a hair "salon."

I was seated quickly. As the woman behind me snipped away at my long, dark hair, I kept my eyes focused on the floor, not wanting to see my reflection in the mirror. Each snip of her scissors caused my heart to beat a little faster.

After cutting what I was sure was every hair off the top of my head, the woman took out a large and frightening object that shot out warm air that she blew onto my wet strands. Once dry, she continued to mess and spray odd potions into my hair as I sat nervously in the seat. By the time she finished, the city was engulfed in darkness, small street lamps the only visible light outside the window.

"Are ye ready?" They were the first words the woman had spoken to me. With my mouth dry, I simply nodded, keeping my eyes squeezed shut as she turned me to face the mirror.

"Open yer eyes, dear. If ye doona like it, it's only hair. It'll grow back."

Her argument was sound. Slowly, I opened my eyes, unable to stop the wide smile that spread across my features as I took in my glorious reflection.

While I was certain I was going to find myself without hair, she'd actually kept a good amount. With the ends lightly curled around my shoulders, each strand of hair seemed to find new life, no longer weighted down.

"Oh, 'tis lovely." I smiled and stood, hesitantly reaching a hand out to pat the woman on the shoulder. Twas a gesture that seemed acceptable in this time, and now that my hair seemed to fit, I thought I could at least make an effort to make my behaviors fit, as well.

"Great. Now, on to make-up and piercing." Isla stood, extending money toward the hairdresser before motioning that I follow her out of the shop.

We found our next stop one block further down, on a street even more dimly lit than the last and situated in between two shops claiming to draw pictures on people's skin. We made our way inside.

Once again, I was thrust into a seat, and the proprietor obeyed Isla's orders and held different shapes and sizes of shiny objects up to my ear. Once Isla found one that satisfied her, I was told to sit back and not move, as there would soon be a prick to my earlobe.

I relaxed, certain that a prick would be no worse than being stuck by a pin while being fitted for a dress. The proprietor squeezed his fingers together over a foreign contraption he'd placed over the lobe of my ear, and I felt the rod of the object pierce my skin. I let out a howl I was sure the Conalls could hear all the way back in 1646.

onall Castle – 1646

"*A*re ye sure that ye wanna go through with it? I willna be able to sleep a wink while ye are both away. I think ye are being foolish, but ye never wish to listen to me." Mary fluttered nervously around the spell room, rambling as she listed reasons why Eoin and Bri should not try and go forward to retrieve Blaire, only stopping when she was interrupted by Adelle, who stood anxiously in the doorway.

"She's right. I miss Blaire, but I'd rather the two of you didn't risk your own lives to go look for her."

The two women continued to rant back and forth, talking more to each other than to Eoin or Bri, each doing their best to proclaim themselves as alpha among the mother and mother-figure duo.

Bri looked over her shoulder at Eoin, who had his arms wrapped around her to hold her close. "They aren't going to stop until we are gone, you know that, right? It's best that we get going. It will take us a few hours to walk to the inn, and we are going to have some explaining to do about your clothing if we run into anyone at the castle or along the road."

"Aye, lass. I suppose ye are right. What are we to tell them again?"

Eoin squeezed Bri tightly, and she sighed in response to the comfort of his warm arms around her. "Well, let's hope that we don't bump into anyone who works at the castle, like a tour guide. If we do, we will just tell them that you wanted to dress up to get into the spirit of things. They will think you're crazy, but any girl that sees you is just going to be so pleased to have the opportunity to gaze upon you shirtless, I doubt they will care much about your sanity."

Bri smiled as he chuckled deeply into her ear. "I doona think that is so, lass. I'm not so uncommon looking."

"Pfff...yeah, whatever." She paused to twist and give him a swift kiss on the lips. "Let's shut these two yappers up and get out of here. You ready?"

"Aye. Do ye wanna get their attention or should I?"

"I'll do it. I know just how to get a response out of Mom." Bri smiled before she shouted, "Adelle!" in her mother's direction. Instantly, her mother's eyes widened and she whipped toward her, awarding Bri with a stern expression.

"What? I know that you didn't just call me 'Adelle,' right? I'm your mother."

Bri stepped away from Eoin and looked up at him. "Told ya," she whispered before moving to pull her mother into a hug. "We're leaving now, Mom. It's going to be fine. Morna's spells seem to be pretty reliable." Bri pulled away from her mother's vice-like embrace and moved over to hug Mary. "Now, both of you try not to worry while we're gone. It may be a few weeks before we return. Just keep yourselves busy."

It was Mary's turn to react. "Do ye not think that I always

keep myself busy? Do ye think I just lie around the castle, trying to dream up things to do?"

Bri rolled her eyes and stepped back so that Eoin could bid both of the women farewell. "No, of course I don't think that, Mary, and you know it," she said. "Now remember, don't let Arran find out where we've gone off to. He'll find out soon enough if Blaire wants to return. But in case she doesn't, I don't want him getting his hopes up."

Both women nodded. When it was clear that Bri and Eoin were about to begin the spell, they quietly retreated from the small room.

Standing in front of the old, faded book, Bri took Eoin's hands. Together they lit the candles and read aloud the words from the book. Momentary shock waves of pain coursed through them. They wrapped their arms around one another and, together, vanished from the room.

*M*uffled voices became audible above their heads. Both groggy and confused, they leaned against the walls of the once familiar room until they found themselves reoriented. Having already made the trip through once, Bri knew instantly the headache Eoin would have and went straight for her mother's backpack, still tucked neatly behind the bench in front of the table, out of sight from the eyes of wandering tourists.

Opening the inner zipper pocket, she pulled out the bottle of Advil and dumped out five round pills into her hand, two for herself and three for her beast of a husband. They had no water, but if either of them were to function, they had to medicate the head trauma that always seemed to occur when travelling through time by way of Morna's spells.

"Here." Blaire moved to stand in front of Eoin, her legs still slightly unsteady and discombobulated. "Put these in your mouth and swallow them. They will help with your headache."

Obligingly, Eoin held open his hand and looked down at the pills questioningly. "What are they, lass? They look too small to do much for my head."

Bri slowly raised his hand to motion for him to put them in his mouth. "Trust me. They'll help. At least it looks like we made it. Look at how old everything in the room is."

Bri smiled as she watched Eoin wander about the room, awestruck. She reached a hand in his direction as she moved to the door leading to the staircase out of the basement. "Did you hear the voices above us just a moment ago? I think they must be conducting a tour. No surprise, since we were able to stop the castle from being destroyed. I'm sure it's quite the tourist attraction today. Which means it's going to be difficult for us to get out of the place unseen."

Eoin winked, and Bri smiled at the playfulness in his eyes. "Aye. I expect since I have ye with me, it shall be impossible. Ye are talented at falling down. I'm certain I will have to scoop ye off the floor at least twice before we make our escape."

Bri leaned her ear against the spell room door, listening for any sign of movement on the other side. "What about you?" she whispered. "You're not so light on your feet yourself. Now, let's go. I don't hear anybody on the other side."

Cautiously, Bri pulled the door open, finding the main basement room empty. As she closed the secret door to the spell room behind them, she could tell that it had remained unfound despite the years of tourism at the castle. The only sign of entrance within the basement was an "employees only" sign that was draped across the floor in front of the staircase leading up and out of the room.

Hesitantly, Bri climbed the stairs and gently pulled at the door. The ridged nature of the door's hinges showed her that not even castle employees went down into the basement very often.

But as luck would have it, just as Eoin had securely shut the spell room door, hiding it from view, they both heard the door at the top of the basement stairs open. Listening to the sound of footsteps descend the staircase, they soon found themselves staring back at a very official-looking castle employee whose eyes widened in shock at the sight of them.

S cotland – *Present Day*

M itsy soon-to-be Fredrickson angrily slammed the car door and stood to smooth her shirt and pants before making her way to the front of the small roadside inn. Her connecting flight out of Chicago had been delayed a whopping six hours, cutting the time that she could spend searching for Bri in Scotland short by almost an entire day.

Not to mention the time it had taken her to rent a car and find a decent map, none of which seemed to show the location of the inn. Hours later, frustrated, tired, and worried sick, Mitsy found herself standing in front of the last place Bri had supposedly been seen.

She hoped Bri was safe, but part of her knew that if she walked into that inn to find her AWOL maid of honor lounging around as if on vacation, she was going to kill her on the spot. Determined to find an answer, she rapped her knuckles against the wooden door with as much authority as she could muster.

The door swung open so quickly she nearly pummeled the head of the old man who now stood before her, smiling. "Come in, lass. Why do ye seem to be in such a hurry? We've plenty of rooms if ye are looking for a place to stay."

Mitsy stepped inside, her angry resolve slipping slightly at the friendliness in the man's eyes. Surely he couldn't be responsible for anything that might've happened to Bri. Stopping just inside the doorway, she said, "I'm not looking for a room. I'm looking for a person. Brielle Montgomery. She supposedly stayed here. She's been missing for some time now, and the police have closed the investigation because they spoke to you and your wife, and you told them that she was fine. She can't be fine. She wouldn't just leave without giving me an explanation." The man's brows creased together, as if he was unsure of how to respond, and Mitsy immediately grew suspicious. "Where is she?"

"Why doona ye follow me into the kitchen, lass, and we can talk about yer friend?"

Mitsy lightly stomped her foot against the ground in an effort to root herself firmly in place. "I don't think so, sir. I think you need to tell me whatever it is you know about Bri right this instant."

"Gwendolyn, can ye come in here, sweetheart? We have a visitor who is looking for Bri." The man paused and, while waiting for his wife to arrive, extended a hand in Mitsy's direction. "My name is Jerry. And ye might be?"

Mitsy didn't accept his hand, only curtly giving her name before his wife rounded the corner from the kitchen and came to stand in front of her. "I'm Mitsy," she said to the older woman. "Now, tell me where Bri is."

Gwendolyn smiled.

"I'm afraid she's not here. She moved to Edinburgh only a few weeks ago. She's working as a maid in a hotel, I believe. If ye like, I can give ye directions to the place."

Shock coursed through Mitsy as she took in the old woman's words. Hotel maid? Moved? Why would Bri suddenly decide to drastically change her life? It didn't make sense. Her voice was shaky when she tried to speak. "Y-Yes. Please. I would appreciate directions."

Holding the small pad in which Gwendolyn had written directions to where Bri was supposedly staying, Mitsy turned and made her way back to the car. She didn't care that she was so tired she could hardly keep her eyes open and so hungry that the sheep in the fields looked appetizing, she was going to find Bri tonight.

———

"Why did ye tell the lass that Bri was in Edinburgh? Doona ye remember that it is Blaire living there?" Jerry looked at his wife with concern, only to be rewarded with a soft smack on his arm.

"O'course I know 'tis Blaire. Doona ye worry about it, dear. The real Bri is on her way to us as we speak. Once she gets here, we will send her in the same direction as Mitsy."

CHAPTER 7

I glanced out of the corner of my eye, watching Mik as he gathered his coat and made his way to the door. Nearing half past ten, we were supposed to remain open until midnight. I had every intention of closing down the pub as soon as Mik left.

He paused at the door and turned to me. "Are ye sure ye doona mind closing alone, Blaire? I know that it was yer turn to leave early, only some of my friends are throwing a party and--"

I held a hand up to stop him. "Aye, 'tis fine. I doona mind."

Smiling, he opened the front door, sending a blast of frigid air through the room. He paused before walking out, and turned to look at me.

"Ye are welcome to stop by after if ye'd like."

Mik didn't wait for my response. As the door shut, I reached behind me for a wet cloth, and hurriedly began wiping down the counters. If the owner found out I'd closed early, I'd be sure to take the blame. I didn't want Mik to get in trouble, but it was Thursday evening and the pub's only customer was the ancient drunkard who had spent every night here since my first evening tending bar.

Once the counter was wiped clean, I circled the tables, gathering glasses to put in the dishwasher. Every time I started the strange machine, I couldn't help but smile. It was a miraculous invention and much more pleasant than the vacuum and other cleaning instruments of this time. It was much more quiet, and the swishing of the water was a sound I found soothing.

Giving the room another glance to ensure that everything was clean and ready for those working the next day's opening shift, I made my way to the telephone hanging on the side wall. Pulling out the number Isla had given me, I called for a taxi. Telephones were a convenience quite useful on evenings like this when I had no one to help me make sure the old drunkard found his way home. But other than those types of occasions, the ease with which people could contact one another in this modern time made me uneasy.

Having grown so accustomed to remaining in constant contact, people in the twenty-first century became anxious too quickly after not hearing from a loved one or friend. It is much easier to wait for news if you know it will be a long time in coming, than to constantly be aware that every second could bring change.

Pushing my musings aside, I walked over to the old man, who now lay slumped over and snoring. I did my best to rouse him from his slumber as I waited for the taxi that would take him home.

---

*A*fter well past twenty-four hours without sleep, Mitsy's exhaustion started to addle her brain. "What do you mean she doesn't work here? I was just told that she did." Well past twenty-four hours without sleep, Mitsy's exhaustion started to idle her brain. With each word that she spoke, she grew more frustrated and had to blink back tears. It took all of her willpower not to throw a temper tantrum in the middle of the small hotel lobby. She glared at the nervous-looking girl behind the front desk.

"I do apologize, miss. I only started last week, and I've never heard of anyone working here by the name of Bri. It's possible that she does, though. Maybe we've never worked the same shift. Give me just a moment, and I'll ask a few of the maids."

"Yes. Please." Mitsy spotted a lounge chair in the corner, made her way to it, and collapsed onto the worn seat. She placed her fingertips on her eyelids, prying them open and staring blankly at the carpet in an effort to stay awake. A hand on her shoulder caused her to jump, poking herself in the eye. "Ouch!" She stood, straightening and pulling at the hem of her shirt before looking up at the person in front of her.

"Sorry, miss," said the front desk clerk, stepping back to allow another young woman to move up alongside her. "This is Isla," she explained, by way of introduction. "She knows the person ye are looking for, but the girl no longer works here, and her name isna Bri."

Isla nodded. "Hello. Is it perhaps Blaire that ye are looking for, miss? Dark hair, blue eyes, terrible maid. I doona know a Bri who has worked here, but Blaire most certainly fits the description."

Mitsy swallowed the lump in her throat and pushed her hair behind her ears as she repressed the frustration building once again inside of her. "No. I'm not looking for someone named Blaire. I'm looking for a Brielle Montgomery. Everybody calls her Bri. She's American. She does have dark hair and blue eyes, but I'd be very surprised if she was a terrible maid. That woman is the most anal, organized, nasty-nice person I know. Now I just spoke with an elderly couple who told me that they'd helped secure her job here. It's very important that I find her."

"Hmm." Isla frowned and shook her head. "I doona know a Bri, miss. The only person that I can think of is Blaire. She wasna American, but her accent was a little odd, and she never told any of us where she came from or why she was here. Do ye think that she could have been your friend and pretending to be someone she isn't? Is she running from something?"

Mitsy sat in the chair once again as the woman's words sunk in. She didn't think that Bri would go to the effort of changing her name and using an accent, but then again she never would have thought that she herself would go traipsing all over Scotland looking for her best friend, either. She gathered her things. "I don't know. Can you tell me where this Blaire is now? It won't hurt for me to meet her and see for myself."

"Sure. She's working at my cousin's pub," said Isla. "It's not far from here. I can point ye in the right direction. I doona know if she's working now, but ye can at least go and check."

Minutes later, after being shown the way by Isla, Mitsy uttered a thank you and took off as quickly as her sleep-deprived body would carry her.

The taxi arrived in just under half an hour, and the old drunk man still sat slumped over a small table at the back of the room. After I agreed to pay the taxi driver double what it would cost to get the man home, he came inside and helped me get the old man into the cab.

Twenty minutes later, I gathered up my empty wallet, put on my coat, and flipped the lights off as I made my way to the front doors to lock up for the night. Due to my bulky gloves, I fumbled to get a grip on the correct key. Finally giving up, I bit the fingertip of one of my gloves, allowing me to slip it off so I could get a better grasp on the slippery keys.

The street around me was dark, and I hurried at my task as best I could, not wanting to linger any longer than necessary. I twisted and pulled on the door handle to ensure it locked, and was just slipping my glove back on when a loud voice to my left caused me to drop the glove and keys.

"Oh my God, Bri! It is you. I am going to freaking kill you! Open that door back up right now, because we are about to have quite the conversation, and I'd rather not freeze to death while doing so."

Not moving to pick up my belongings, I stared back at the strange, red-haired woman. The only word I'd been able to understand that she'd spoken was the name Bri, and I wasnn't sure of how to deal with the woman's assumption that I was Adelle's daughter. She seemed to know my look-alike quite well.

"Oh. Surprised to see me, are you?" the woman said, her voice oozing sarcasm. "What? Did you really think you could just skip out on your entire life and not expect anyone to come looking for you? You weren't that much of a loner, Bri. There are people who care about you. I care about you! Now, quit staring at me like I'm the one who's lost my mind. Open that door, or I will open it myself."

In an effort to allow myself a few moments to think about my best course of action, I bent to retrieve my glove and the keys to the pub. Then I obeyed the woman's orders by opening the door. Assuming she would follow, I made my way inside and flipped on the lights. I knew I couldn't pretend to be Bri. If this woman knew her well, it would be impossible to fool her.

Turning to her, I said, "I'm not Bri. My name is Blaire." I paused, guilt at causing her pain and confusion making me shift nervously.

The woman's eyes bulged, and her face reddened. "You have got to be joking. You do realize that coming to find you has cost me several months' salary, don't you? That's something I really can't afford considering I've been busy planning a wedding for the last year and a half. Or did you forget about that, too?"

I wrinkled my nose, knowing whatever I said was going to upset her. "I'm verra sorry, miss, but I truly doona know who ye are."

"Sorry? Well then. I'm sorry for what I'm about to do, as well. But I bet that when I'm finished, you'll remember who I am and who you are just fine."

She lunged toward me, but I managed to move quickly out of her path, beginning an odd dance of lunge and dash around the empty room.

CHAPTER 8

*P*resent Day – Conall Castle

*B*ri glanced uncomfortably at her half-dressed husband before turning back to face the shocked custodian. "Hello," she said, smiling as sweetly as she could and reaching for Eoin's hand. "We were just leaving," she told the silent man, pulling Eoin toward the stairs behind them.

She hoped they would be able to exit without further explanation. Her mother had told her once that if you walked with authority and pretended like you were somewhere you were supposed to be, people were less likely to question your behavior. It had worked well for her mother, allowing Adelle to ransack through more museum displays than Bri could count. However, she sensed she would not have the same success as her mother, and knew she was right when the custodian moved to stand in front of her, blocking their exit from the basement.

"Now, I know that ye both must have seen the 'Do Not Enter'

sign on the front of this door. What made ye think the sign dinna apply to the two of ye?"

Eoin started to speak, but Bri quickly threw an elbow into his ribs to silence him. The feeling of his bare chest against her skin gave her an idea. Before allowing herself to think it through, she threw her right arm over Eoin's shoulder and snuggled in close to reach over and kiss his cheek. "I'm sorry, sir. You see, we are visiting the area on our honeymoon, and the castle is just so romantic. We are having a hard enough time keeping our hands off each other as it is. When our tour group walked by here, I just decided to take the opportunity to slip away for a few moments with my new husband." Not waiting for the man to respond, Bri turned and pressed herself up against Eoin, kissing him hard on the mouth.

She allowed the kiss to go on for a few moments, intent on making her point to the castle employee. Finally, hearing the man clear his throat, Bri pulled away from an open-mouthed, grinning Eoin.

"Ah, well," said the custodian, "um . . . there are certain places for such things, and this isna one of them. I should have ye escorted out immediately, but seeing as ye are newlyweds, I'll cut the two of ye a break, aye? But I doona want to catch ye somewhere that ye shouldn't be again." He frowned at Eoin. "And why are ye not wearing a shirt, man?"

Again, Bri nudged an elbow of warning into her husband's ribs. She waved a hand flippantly in the air. "Oh. That. It's a costume. He wanted to, ya know, get into the spirit of things."

The man didn't respond, only moved out of their way so they could exit the stairwell. Shutting the door behind them, Bri started to thank the custodian but stopped as the man chuckled once, muttering "Americans" under his breath before shaking his head and turning to leave them alone in the empty hallway.

"Lass, I know I agreed that ye would be in charge during our journey here, but do ye really think that was the best way to handle it? That man thinks that we are both mad, and the way ye dinna allow me to speak, why he must think I'm a mute."

Bri laughed, slightly shocked at her own behavior. "I'm sorry. I didn't know what to do. When I felt your bare chest behind me, it was the only thing that popped in my head. But what does it matter, anyway? It worked, didn't it? Now, let's get out of here before another tour passes by. I don't want to have to explain your clothing again." Dragging her husband along behind her, they made their way out of the castle without seeing another soul.

*E*oin frowned at his wife. "Do ye think Blaire will still be here? If she wanted a different life for herself, this hardly seems the place."

Bri knocked on the door of the inn before answering his question. "No, I doubt that she is, but maybe they'll know where to find her. Either way, it might be a bit of a tricky situation. They thought that Blaire was me, so I'm not sure how we are going to explain my sudden appearance, not to mention yours."

The door opened, startling both of them. Before Bri could utter a hello, she was pulled into Jerry's rail-thin arms.

"Bri, it's good to see ye again, lass. And Eoin, ye sure are quite the big lad, are ye not? My wife will be quite pleased to see ye. Now, come inside." Jerry waved them into the living room and shouted toward the kitchen. "They're here, dear."

Bri was certain her mouth hung open as she glanced back at Eoin, whose pinched brows and wide eyes matched her own. Once seated, Jerry excused himself, and Bri leaned over to whisper to Eoin, "Did he just call you by your name? How could he possibly know that?"

Eoin answered absent-mindedly as he glanced around the room. "I doona know. Bri, how is the room lit? I doona think the flames above our heads would be easily lit or put out."

Bri smiled and pointed to the light switch on the wall. "They aren't flames. It's electricity. All you have to do to turn them on is flip that tiny switch over there. Flipping it in the other direction will turn the lights off."

"Ye canna mean it? What a change from our dark, candlelit rooms. Tell me, will we be alive to see lights such as this?"

"No, I'm afraid not. You'll see lots of amazing things while we are here, and I can't wait to watch you discover them, but first..." Bri paused as Jerry entered the room, Gwendolyn trailing him. She stood to give the old woman a hug, then returned to the couch and sat again.

"Bri, you don't need to worry about how you are going to explain your situation to us," said Gwendolyn. "We know that while you were here with your mother at the beginning, it was Blaire for most of the time. In fact, I believe I have some things I must explain to both of you. But first, I'd like to kiss my nephew."

Before Bri or Eoin could react, she moved across the room, grabbed Eoin by both cheeks, and brought him near to her, kissing him on the forehead.

Bri's mind reeled at the spectacle, and only Jerry's voice brought her back to her senses.

"Ach, lassie. That's not even half of it. Ye best settle in and prepare yerself for some interesting news."

*I*t was almost eleven when Bri and Eoin parked the car they'd borrowed from Jerry in front of the pub where Blaire supposedly now worked. The lights were on inside, and while she couldn't see Blaire through the windows, Bri hoped that their search would end here, and their evening of overwhelming surprises would be over.

"Are you ready?" Bri asked Eoin as they made their way to the entrance. "Blaire knows you, so I think it might be best if you speak to her first." She reached for the door handle but paused at the touch of Eoin's hand on her forearm.

"Did ye believe her story, Bri? Do ye think 'tis possible that she really is my Aunt Morna?"

"Yes, I do. After all that we've been through, I find it very difficult to be surprised anymore." She tilted her head to one side, studying his strained expression. "Are you all right? Does it upset you to know that she's been here all this time, while letting you all think she'd died?"

He shook his head. "No. I only wish my father was here to see her. He missed her dearly. He'd be so pleased to know that she is loved and happy. He was the only one around her that dinna fear her witchcraft."

"Well, it seems your father was right. I don't think there is any reason to fear Morna. I, for one, will be forever grateful for all she has done. I wouldn't have you otherwise." Bri leaned in briefly to lightly kiss Eoin on the cheek. "Now, let's get in there and see to Blaire."

"Aye, I doona like cars. Nothing should be able to move so quickly. 'Tisna natural."

Bri laughed as they exited the vehicle and walked to the door of the pub. "You go first. I'm nervous to see my lookalike." She gently nudged Eoin's back, urging him to try the lock.

"Aye, fine. But I doona believe ye should be nervous. I should, however. I doona expect the lass will be too pleased to see me."

The door was unlocked, and they stepped inside to the chaotic scene of overturned chairs and tables. Blaire lay sprawled in the corner, straddled by some red-haired woman whose face they couldn't see. The two women screamed incoherently at one another.

"Eoin!" Bri exclaimed. "Help her! Get that woman off of her. What is she doing?"

Eoin bolted toward Blaire while Bri approached cautiously, standing back to watch as her husband separated the two women.

Blaire stood quickly, glancing down at her disheveled clothing, brushing dust off the bottom of her pants. Bri knew that her lookalike had yet to see her, or to recognize the man holding her assailant. "Thank ye. The woman is mad," Blaire said, out of breath.

The woman in question screamed in protest and threw her head back, sending the red curls that covered her face backward, revealing her face.

Bri gasped aloud in recognition as she rushed toward her old friend. "Mitsy?"

"Bri?" In an effort to escape Eoin's hold on her, Mitsy lunged, and Blaire looked up for the first time since they'd entered the pub.

"Eoin?" Blaire gasped.

CHAPTER 9

I'd witnessed many surprising things since arriving in this century, but none had shocked me more than seeing my ex-fiancé staring back at me, and a woman who looked like my duplicate standing beside him. I knew she must be Bri.

When I made the decision to stay here, I felt certain I would never see anyone from my past life ever again. To find Eoin standing before me now meant that Morna's spells were not as close-ended as Adelle and I had originally thought.

When the woman who had attacked me saw Bri, she shrieked and chaos ensued. Bri shrieked, too, and a tremor of shock reverberated throughout the room. Only Eoin remained calm. He eventually quieted everyone by slamming his fist down so hard against the table that the entire room seemed to shake.

"Quiet, all three of ye!" he boomed. "It has been a long day, and I doona think I can take such noise any longer."

Recognizing the seriousness of his tone, the three of us quieted instantly. But only a moment passed before the redheaded mad woman spoke again.

"Somebody better tell me what's going on here, or I'm going to lose it on every single one of you." Her voice trembled, and she pointed a shaky finger in Bri's direction. "Now, you are Bri, right? If you tell me you're not, I swear I will jump on top of you like I did this one." She nodded her head at me, adding, "How did I not know you have a twin?"

I leaned against the wall behind me, confused as to the circumstances surrounding Eoin and Bri's arrival here, as well, yet quite entertained with the exchange taking place between the two women.

"She's not my twin," said Bri. "I'm not related to Blaire at all, as far as I know." She stepped closer to the other woman, her brows knitting together. "Mitsy, what are you doing here?"

Anger flashed in the redhead's face. A redhead who now had the name of Mitsy. For a moment, I was certain she was going to try and escape Eoin's restraining arms again.

"What am I doing here?" Mitsy hissed. "You have got to be kidding me! What are *you* doing here? God, Bri, I thought you were dead! You've been gone for months with no word or explanation. Your trip to Scotland with your mother was only supposed to last a few weeks. I've been trying to locate you ever since the police stopped their investigation. You're supposed to be in my wedding, Bri! I can't believe you just left everything. Were you really just not going to show up without any excuse whatsoever?"

Mitsy collapsed into a fit of sobs, and Eoin relaxed his hold on her. Bri moved in to comfort her friend, gathering Mitsy into her arms. "I'm so angry at you!" Mitsy choked out through her tears. "If I thought I could get away with it, I'd kill you myself."

Bri ushered her friend away from Eoin and me. "I know," she said in a soothing voice. "Let's move over here out of the way so we can talk in private. I need to explain what's happened, and Eoin and Blaire need a chance to get reacquainted."

"I know. Let's move over here and talk so that I can explain what's happened to you. It will give Eoin and Blaire a chance to get reacquainted."

As the two women moved toward the bar, I didn't miss the apologetic look Bri shot in Eoin's direction, presumably for leaving him alone with me. Without doubt, my relationship with Eoin had always been slightly contentious, but only because I didn't want to marry him. If I'd known him under any other circumstance, I suspected we would've gotten along just fine. I found myself a little embarrassed to know that Bri had heard of my terrible behavior toward him.

"Eoin." I nodded once, determined to let him initiate any conversation. Always the gentlemen, he moved to pick up my hand and kiss it lightly before stepping away again.

"Blaire, ye look well. Do ye enjoy being here in this time, lass? It's verra different from our own. Are ye happy?"

His question surprised me, and I couldn't help but wonder if perhaps I wasn't doing as good a job at looking happy as I had hoped. Truth was, I was lonely. And while I loved the independence women enjoyed in this time, I missed my home. But I knew it was most likely impossible for me to return. Even if I could, I didn't think I could stand the heartache that would come with being near Arran and knowing I was unwanted.

It took me a moment too long to answer Eoin, and I knew he could read the untruth behind my words. "Aye. O'course I'm happy. Why wouldna I be? Why are ye here, Eoin? I'm verra surprised to see ye."

Eoin chuckled. "Aye, I suppose ye are. I'm surprised to find myself here, as well. Bri wished to come to take care of some things that were left unfinished from her life here. I wouldna let her go alone. If something happened, I doona think I could go back to a life without her."

"I'm glad that ye are happy, Eoin. Is all well with yer family? Have ye heard from my father?" I didn't mention Arran, but something in Eoin's eyes made me wonder if he knew it was Arran I was asking about. Was it possible that Eoin knew about what had occurred between his brother and me? If so, perhaps Arran had not closed his heart so completely to me. The thought gave way for a small trickle of hope to rise within me, one which I quickly pushed down while I waited for Eoin's response.

He waved me to a table in the corner of the room. Pointing toward Bri and Mitsy, he said, "It looks as if they may be a while. Let us sit, and I'll tell ye all that has happened while ye have been away."

I nodded and followed, glancing quickly at the two women visiting at the bar. As I watched them, I remembered the shocked expression on Bri's face when she realized the woman Eoin was holding back was Mitsy. Bri hadn't known her friend would be here. Eoin had lied. They had not come to the pub so that Bri could give Mitsy an explanation, they'd come here looking for me.

"*D*id you tell her why we came here?" Bri led the way to their hotel room as Eoin slowly followed, stopping every so often to stare at something new that fascinated him. Several hours after arriving at the pub, they'd all left together, first dropping Blaire off at her apartment, and next, securing two hotel rooms for the three of them just across the street from Blaire's place of residence. With Mitsy shut away in her room for the evening, Bri and Eoin were finally able to discuss what had occurred over the last few hours.

"I dinna tell her all of why we came here. I told her ye needed to see to some things ye'd left unfinished, but I dinna tell her that we'd come to see if she would return home."

Bri stopped in front of their room and pulled the plastic key card from her pocket. Smiling, she extended it Eoin's direction. "Here. You see that slot above the handle? Stick this card in there and then slowly pull it out. It will unlock the door."

It took him three tries but Bri remained patient, enjoying the look of awe that radiated from her husband's face. Once inside, she decided to tell him the news she'd dreaded sharing with him since they'd left the pub.

"Well, I suppose it's fine that you haven't told her the other reason we came here just yet. You'll have plenty of time to do that."

She heard her husband stop playing with the toilet in the bathroom, and she knew she'd caught his attention. "What do ye mean by that, lass? Now that ye have spoken with yer friend, we should be able to return home in only a few days, aye?"

Bri shook her head and turned a guilty face toward her husband. "No. I'm afraid not. You and Blaire are going to have the next week all to yourselves. I made a promise over a year ago that I would be Mitsy's maid of honor. I'm leaving with her tomorrow to go back to the States for her wedding."

CHAPTER 10

onall Castle - 1646

*T*ormod Kinnaird left the clan gathering more determined than ever to find a way to take over as laird. In his mind, the title was his by right. He was the eldest son of Ramsay Kinnaird's younger brother, but a bastard son, and therefore unrecognized as a true Kinnaird by all but his mother and sister.

The same meeting had been held every night since the death of his uncle, and everyone grew restless as little progress was made in determining the best way to declare a new laird. Many members of the clan wished to return home and wait to declare a new leader, but the majority of people knew this would leave the clan without protection and would make them look weak in the eyes of neighboring clans—a sure way to invite further conflict and violence.

The only decision they'd all agreed upon was that Edana would not be placed out of her home, which left Tormod to assume that the new laird would marry Edana. Only a few men remained unmarried within the clan. Although he didn't know for sure if Edana would be given any choice in who she married, he intended to make sure that he would be her first choice.

Though improper for him to be in the castle's bedchamber hallway at this time of evening with Eoin Conall away and his drunk of a brother left to manage things, Tormod was almost certain he would be able to sneak into Edana's room unnoticed.

He had seen Edana enter the room at the end of the hallway enough times during their stay here to know that it was hers. He stood in front of the door, unsure whether to knock or to try the handle. The sound of footsteps down the hallway caught his attention. Humming accompanied each step, and he knew it was the castle's head maid, Mary; he believed that was her name. If she saw him, it was unlikely that she would say anything. Even if she did, who was likely to take the word of such a lowly servant?

Tormod didn't want to alarm her; it was best that the maid not see his true character right away. He knocked softly, hoping that Edana hadn't already retired for the evening.

She answered quickly, and he found himself unsure of how best to explain his unexpected arrival at her door. "Edana, how are ye this evening? I was passing by yer door and thought I would check on ye."

Her pale blonde hair hung loose about her shoulders. Her beady green eyes peered back at him, questioning without asking aloud why he was there. She was shy, or at least she did a fine job of feigning shyness. He'd been around her enough, studied her enough, to notice how she behaved when she believed no one was watching. The girl had far more fire and bite than she let on.

While many people who possessed the same fiery spirit were fueled by their immense passion for life, he recognized that Edana's fire came from a different source. Her fire raged out of an underlying malice for everything and everyone around her;

something that she'd inherited from her father, no doubt. He knew she did her best to hide her true nature, but he wasn't bothered by it. Tormod held the same feelings of malice for all those around him, as well, and he could see it in her eyes even now.

He smiled and glanced quickly down either side of the hallway before speaking again. "May I come in? I doona wish to be seen outside your chamber this late in the evening."

Edana looked down at her feet, and then silently stepped away from the door, allowing Tormod entry into the room.

"What are ye doing here, Tormod? Ye shouldna be in this part of the castle." She spoke with her back toward him as she walked away, leaving him to stand just inside the doorway as she took a seat near the hearth.

Slowly, he moved to sit across from her. But when she didn't protest, he sat down, instead, by her side. "I wanted to see ye. I always want to see ye, but I've only just gathered the courage to do so."

"What? Why, I've never seen ye so much as look at me before." Her voice came out high and squeaky.

Tormod recognized that this was not part of her façade. She was genuinely surprised to hear his explanation. His confidence growing, he scooted closer, reaching over to grasp her hand. "Aye. I've looked at ye many times before, lass, and I see ye now, as well." He rubbed his thumb gently back and forth across the top of her hand until she moved away and stood, pushing her hair from her face in a nervous gesture. Making her way to the door, she opened it and motioned for him to leave.

"Ye canna mean it," Edana snapped. "I doona wish to be toyed with. 'Tis not enough that I just lost my father, and that I'm now forced to live in the home of the very people who took him from me? Do ye wish to tease me, as well? I willna allow it. Now,

65

leave." She pointed toward the door and Tormod stood, realizing he'd just learned all he needed to know about the lass.

Not only did Edana hate most everyone around her, she also held herself in great contempt. Only a woman with a very low sense of self-worth would immediately assume that a suitor at her door this late in the evening was there to belittle her. Edana's feelings toward herself would serve him well. It was easy to make self-loathing women fall in love. In the hopes of receiving the admiration they denied themselves, they would heedlessly throw their heart at the first suitor to ask for it.

Passing her on his way out the door, he paused quickly to steal a kiss. The whispery sigh that escaped her lips was not one of protest, and he smiled as he leaned forward to whisper in her ear. "I will never tease ye, Edana. I intend to make ye mine."

He didn't give her a chance to respond, turning quickly to make his leave. He knew his visit had been successful. He'd left the poor lass wanting more, with her heart beating wildly in her chest. In a week's time, she'd want no other man but him. Of that he was sure.

Three Days Later

When a knock sounded at his chamber door, Arran rolled drowsily out of bed, cursing Kip for creating so many tasks for him to complete in the stables that day. He knew it was unusual for someone in his position to work in the stables, but he didn't care. Kip had worked him from dawn to dusk, and although Arran complained, he knew it was a good thing. Staying busy was the only thing that kept the drinking at bay and the pain in his heart at a safe distance.

He threw open the door to find out who felt the need to disturb him so late in the evening, and he had to blink several times to make sure his vision was clear when he saw Mary standing in his doorway.

"Mary? What are ye doing? Ye should've been in bed hours ago. Ye work too much as it is."

Mary waved a hand in dismissal at Arran's words as she stepped inside without waiting to be invited. "I doona need ye telling me when I should be in bed, and I doona work too much. I work just the proper amount. 'Tis only that ye work too little that ye think anything more than that is too much."

"Ah. O'course ye are right, Mary." Arran knew better than to argue with her, and so he simply smiled and crossed his arms as he prepared to hear what she had to say. "Now, what do ye need? Ye havena been in my bedchamber this late since I was a wee lad."

"Ye are right, and I see ye havena changed yer bad habits at all. Ye still doona have enough common sense to check and make sure ye are properly clothed before ye invite company into yer room. For goodness sakes, cover yerself. I think ye have blinded me." She shielded her eyes dramatically as Arran glanced down at his entirely naked self.

"Ach, Mary! I'm verra sorry." Scrambling, he reached for something to cover himself, finally deciding to simply sit on the edge of the bed so that he could pull the blanket across his lap.

"Doona apologize, lad. 'Tis not like I havena seen a man naked before. Why, I used to clean that little backside of yers when ye were only a wee laddie."

Arran rolled his eyes, wishing Mary would spit out her news so he could return to a peaceful slumber. "Let's not talk about my backside. What's brought ye here?"

"Ah, right." Mary stopped grinning and faced him head on. "I'm verra worried about Edana."

"Aye? Why?" Arran was awake now. He'd been worried about the lass, too, but he didn't understand why Mary would be. He straightened up in the bed, eager to hear her concerns.

"For the past three evenings, I have seen Ramsay's nephew sneaking into Lady Edana's room late at night. It isna proper for him to visit her after dark."

"Ye are right; it is not. But they are our guests, and I doona think 'tis our place to instruct them on how to behave themselves. Besides, I doubt he is doing anything to the lass she wouldna want him to." He believed his own words, but he couldn't deny how uncomfortable the thought made him. He wasn't jealous of Tormod. He didn't care about Edana in that way. But he had seen the lad interacting with some of his men, and Arran had an uneasy feeling when around him.

"No, I doona think he is hurting her, Arran," Mary explained. "I think he is using her so he can become laird. Ye know that our visitors decided that whomever becomes laird should marry Edana. I believe he is trying to make her want to do just that, which would be fine except for I doona think Tormod is a good man. Not even much better than Edana's father."

"Aye, I agree with ye, Mary. I doona like the lad either." Arran lay back on his bed, gathering the blankets to cover himself, drumming his fingers back and forth across his forehead as he tried to think of how to best proceed.

Only one plausible solution crossed his mind. Although the idea didn't thrill him, it was the only way he could come up with that might keep his new friend from entering a horrible marriage. With no hope of his own true love coming back to him, what did it matter whom he married anyway? He sat up. "I know what I shall do, Mary. We shall have a series of games to test the strength and leadership of all the men who enter. The winner shall marry Edana and become laird of Kinnaird's old territory."

Mary drew her brows together, and Arran knew she did not yet understand his plan. "Aye, fine. But how do ye think ye shall get the Kinnaird Clan to agree to such an arrangement, and what if Tormod wins? That will do nothing to keep her from him."

"They will agree because they are all eager to name a new laird. If they do not, they will no longer have the hospitality of staying on our land. And Tormod willna win."

Mary's scrunched eyebrows rose in question. "And just how do ye know that? He's quite a strong-looking lad."

"Tormod willna win because I plan to enter. I will win and marry Edana myself."

CHAPTER 11

*S*cotland – *Present Day*

I was unsure of how Bri and Eoin convinced me to leave with them. It certainly meant losing another job, and I didn't have any other friends that could help me in obtaining another one once I returned to Edinburgh.

I continued to question my decision as I sat in the back of the small, cramped car next to Bri's friend, Mitsy, who had thankfully settled down. I was sure she thought us all mad. How could anyone not after hearing our story? All the same, she was no longer hysterical, and it was undeniable that she'd been in desperate need of a good night's sleep. She looked much better, even quite striking, with her long, red curls fixed nicely, no longer matted down by tears.

As we pulled up in front of the all-too-familiar inn near the castle, I realized that it was a potent mixture of fear and hope that had caused me to agree to stay here with Eoin for the next week. I'd sworn to myself that I wouldn't return to the inn ever again, and I was terrified to do so now, but I was even more terrified of letting this opportunity slip away. I'd suspected last evening in the pub that there was more to Bri and Eoin's visit to this time than Bri's desire to finish some things she'd left undone. Somehow their visit involved me.

My suspicions were confirmed this morning when they asked me to leave town for a week to keep Eoin company and watch over him while Bri and Mitsy left for Mitsy's wedding. Eoin was more than capable of taking care of himself, especially if he was staying with Jerry and Gwendolyn. Or was it Morna? None of us was sure of how to refer to the magical innkeeper anymore. Something remained that Eoin wanted to discuss with me, and my curiosity over that something was enough for me to leave my position in Edinburgh and run toward uncertainty once again.

It seemed likely that Eoin's news might only break my heart further and make me wish I'd remained in Edinburgh. He'd not said much about my father when I'd asked him. Perhaps he was ill or had discovered that I was gone. I hoped he hadn't. I wouldn't be able to bear the guilt of knowing I'd caused my father such pain.

But what if it was something else? What if now that Eoin was married to Bri, Arran wanted me to return home to be with him? The thought made my stomach flutter excitedly, but just as quickly, it turned to an uncomfortable churn as I realized what I knew must be true. Arran didn't want me to return. He probably didn't care that I was gone. If he did, he would have come here himself. He had far too much pride to allow his brother to make such a request of me.

The car had been parked for some time, and everyone else was unloading their belongings as I remained in the back seat, a familiar depression gliding over me as my latest realization drained away all the hope I'd had of Eoin's news being good.

After this week, I would return to the city, jobless once more, and I would start again.

My own reflection in the window startled me, and I jumped as Bri lightly knocked against the window. "Come on inside, Blaire. They have food laid out for you and Eoin. Mitsy and I have to be on our way to the airport. Our flight is in a couple of hours."

Doing my best to manage a smile, I apologized and joined the others inside. Shortly after, Bri and Mitsy drove away, leaving me to wallow in my nerves over what sad news Eoin had yet to share with me.

ustin, TX

*A*s the song came to its end, Bri smiled at her dance partner, pulling him in for a hug. "Thank you, Daniel. You're a wonderful dancer."

"It was my pleasure, dear." The man, forty years her senior, kissed her hand before showing her back to her seat. "And you're right. I am a wonderful dancer. If we'd only been able to go on our date, you would know that already."

Bri laughed as she sat down at the now empty table. All of those seated next to her were out on the dance floor. "My loss."

Daniel winked and tipped his head as he glided back onto the dance floor, no doubt looking for the next beautiful girl he could impress with his dancing skills. Bri smiled to herself as she thought back on the night, which seemed like so many months ago, when she'd been set up on a blind date with Daniel. Her mother's sudden arrival had kept the date from ever beginning.

But thinking back on the shock she'd experienced when first laying eyes on Daniel and realizing his age, the moments of awkwardness that had followed, Bri was reminded that she had some choice words to share with Mitsy's groom.

It had been Mitsy's new husband, Brian, who'd arranged the blind date, and the lack of sense in the match did nothing to help Bri's judgment of him. Something about Brian that she couldn't identify had always bothered her. But tonight was not the time or place to chide the groom. Due to her plans to return to Scotland and, thereafter, back to the seventeenth century the following day, Bri suspected she was just going to have to let this one slide.

Not that she would be able to find the groom to speak to him if she wanted to. The last time she saw him had been at the beginning of the reception during the cutting of the cake and the first dance. Since then, Mitsy singly navigated the crowds of guests eager to congratulate the happy couple. From the beaming smile on Mitsy's face, it didn't seem that she'd taken note of her husband's absence.

Deciding she could go for a restroom break and perhaps for a little groom search and rescue mission, Bri stood and left the reception hall. Arriving at the women's restroom, she was met by the unfortunate staffer who had been dealt the dreadful task of cleaning up some tipsy wedding guest's puke.

"Sorry," said the young woman. "I don't think you want to come in here right now, but if you go to the end of the hall on the right, there's an office. If you enter, there's a bathroom connected to it on the other side. It's fine if you want to use it since you're part of the wedding party. I should have this mess cleaned up for the other guests shortly."

"Thank you, I think I'll do that."

Making her way down the hall, Bri found that her need to use the restroom lessened as a suspicious noise drifted from behind the office door. Upon reaching it, she pressed her ear up against the wooden surface and heard a deep male voice, followed by a feminine giggle.

To Bri's dismay, between giggles, the woman addressed the man by name: Brian.

---

*B*ri fled before her presence on the other side of the office door was discovered. Back at the reception, she quickly downed several glasses of champagne as she tried to decide what she should do.

In the end, she watched her best friend, laughing and beaming as she moved through the reception hall, and knew that while she couldn't bring herself to tell Mitsy so soon after the wedding what she'd heard, she also didn't trust herself *not* to say anything.

She approached her dear friend on the dance floor, made an excuse of feeling sick, and then hugged Mitsy's neck hard. Fighting back tears, Bri hopped into a taxi that would take her back to her hotel.

Chances were she'd never see her friend again, but she wanted to leave Mitsy the option of a new life if she decided she wanted it one day, after she learned the truth about her louse of a husband. Mitsy would eventually; Bri was certain. She only wished that she could be here for her when she did.

When she spotted a post office ahead, Bri knocked on the plastic panel behind the taxi driver to get his attention. She motioned toward the post office. "Can we stop here for a minute before continuing on to the airport? I need to run inside and get a stamp so I can put something in the mail before I leave."

"Sure thing. Meter's running." The driver pulled to the curb.

Climbing out of the cab, Bri walked inside with a heavy heart, hoping with every footstep that if Mitsy needed it, she would be able to believe the words she'd written and mailed the letter to her.

CHAPTER 12

*S*cotland - 1646

*T*ormod's eyes locked with hers as Edana watched him rise from yet another victory, this time in the sword competition. She shivered beneath her clothes at the tingly rush that cascaded over her. She was in love. She could say so without hesitation. Only a week ago, her future had seemed bleak, wrought with uncertainty and a plan for vengeance that she didn't know how to carry out on her own. Now, with Tormod by her side, happiness no longer seemed so impossible.

He loved her, as well, although he'd yet to tell her so. She knew it by the way he treated her. Edana instantly felt she could trust him, and had quickly told him about her true feelings toward the Conalls and her desire to destroy them. She'd expected him to reprimand her, tell her how wrong she was to think that way, but instead, he'd expressed his own hatred. Together, they'd plotted all they could do to destroy the powerful family once they were married and Tormod was laird.

Now, all that stood in their way was the final round of the so-called games that Arran had dreamed up. She found it sickening that her clansmen had so easily agreed to trust her future to a contest. Only a group of men would be so thoughtless. When Arran put the idea to the clan, she'd openly voiced her misgivings on the proposal. However, with the men eager to return home and with no better solutions themselves, they all boisterously agreed to Arran's plan, throwing aside all thought or concern for her feelings.

The only thing that had calmed her was Tormod's reassurance that he would win the competition for her. And she believed that he would. He was close to doing so already. Only one more person would Tormod have to best, and that was by far the most surprising revelation that came out of Arran's idea.

Not only had Arran stood before her clansmen suggesting how to choose their leader, a move that she saw as highly inappropriate and insulting to their intelligence, but he had also asked the clansmen to grant him permission to enter the contest. The people of their clan had worked and lived together for decades and, in time, they would have been more than capable of solving their problem of leadership on their own.

Arran had moved into a lengthy speech, vowing that if he won, as he obviously thought he would, he would be a fair and strong leader, unlike Edana's father. Each word was another dagger intended to destroy any respect her clansmen might have had for her father. Each word stoked the fire of hatred that burned within her for Arran and all of the Conalls, each of them so self-assured in the righteousness of their actions.

To her utter dismay, her clansmen had wholeheartedly welcomed Arran for entrance, many boasting that they would be rooting for him to win, few even questioning the purpose of the competition. Why not just name Arran laird now?

What a fool Arran was. He thought he could trick her into

liking him with his kind words and feigned concern for her wellbeing. It was even more foolish still for him to have such utter confidence in his ability to win her and her territory as his prize. Tormod would never allow it, and if he did, Edana was certain she would kill herself before marrying a Conall.

With archery being the only competition left, Edana stood to go in search of her beloved. She wanted to steal a kiss from the man she would soon call her husband and wish him luck.

———

ormod stood in the corner of his tent. Hunched over, he carefully examined each of his arrows, looking for any inconsistency, any warp in the wood that might impact his shot. Archery was his strength, but he knew Arran was masterful with a bow, as well. He could leave no room for error if he wanted to become laird. The title was within his grasp. He would be laird by nightfall. Then in a few short weeks, his marriage to Edana would be bound with consummation. He could finally end the dreadful task of pretending to like the disgusting wretch.

The rustle of fabric to his left caused him to spin, eager to see who was entering. He'd asked to be left alone so he could concentrate in silence before the last challenge. His sister entered, and he was not surprised that it would be she who gave no credence to his wishes.

"Fia, why are ye here?"

She ignored his question and moved over to his arrows, grabbing one as she raised it in question to him. "Do ye think ye can win?"

The question angered him, and he ripped the arrow out of her hand before continuing, "Aye, I can and I will. Do ye not think so?"

"I do think that ye can. Tis only, I doona think that ye should."

Tormod couldn't believe what she was saying to him. Fia was just as eager as he for their family to gain a place of leadership once again. She, too, had been denied her birthright due to the sins of their parents. "Why would ye say such a thing, Fia? Tis within our grasp now. We will finally be allowed in the castle that should have always been our home."

"Aye, and we shall be. But doona do it today, brother. The people of our clan want Arran to win today. If ye defeat him, they will only resent ye. Claim the lairdship in a way that will earn the respect of our people."

Tormod shook his head, confused and angry at his sister's suggestion. "How would I claim the role once Arran is named laird?"

"Ye watch him, stay close to him, and find a truth that ye can distort into a believable lie. Make the people believe that their precious laird has perpetrated whatever crime of which ye decide to make him guilty. Then it will be much easier for ye to take over as laird. Ye will have earned the trust of our people, and ye may be able to get rid of Edana in the process, as well. I know ye doona wish to be married to the lass."

Tormod paced the room, shaken by the thought of giving up everything within his grasp. He tightened his jaw as he turned to send his sister away. "Ye are right. I doona wish to marry Edana, but there are other ways to dispose of the lass once I am laird. I willna give this up, and if ye wish to be moved to the castle once I am laird, ye willna ask it of me again. Now leave at once."

He turned his back and waited for his sister to leave, tightening his fists as her last words caused him to vibrate with rage.

"As ye wish, but ye will regret this Tormod, and ye will see that I was right."

*T*ormod had just shot his seventh of the required ten arrows. Now it was Arran's turn, and as he drew his seventh and sent it soaring into the center of the target, Tormod didn't miss the roar of his clansmen. Their scores remained tied. With each perfect shot of Tormod's own, Arran matched it. If the routine continued, the two would have to shoot well beyond ten arrows to declare a winner.

Drawing back, Tormod released another flawless shot, quickly turning to take in the crowd that remained mostly silent. His sister was right. There was no denying that the well wishes of his own clansmen lay with his rival. It would be a difficult lairdship if he took over as leader without the support of his people.

Edana would be furious, but he knew he could comfort her with his lies. He would talk her into working with him, and perhaps it would be even easier to destroy Arran if he had an ally that shared Arran's bed.

With Arran sending another perfect shot that matched his own, Tormod drew his bow and jerked his body at the last minute so that his arrow went flying wildly to the side, missing the target completely.

He would allow Arran to be laird for now, but it would be a short-lived reign. Tormod wasted no time in contemplating a dozen ways to destroy the doomed Conall.

CHAPTER 13

*S*cotland – *Present Day*

*B*ri was due back at the inn today, and I still had no idea what Eoin wished to speak with me about. We'd spent the week listening to stories told by Jerry and Morna, who finally had asked that we call her by her real name.

She was a vivid storyteller, and we all enjoyed listening to the adventures of Eoin's father, Alasdair, and my own father when they were growing up. It was a pleasure to watch Eoin discover the aunt he hardly remembered and had envisioned in his mind as a very different woman than she actually was. Her spells and magic were just a small part of this lively, funny, warm woman, and it was easy to see why Alasdair had adored his sister so much, when so many others had feared her.

It was the first morning Eoin and I had spent alone together. Jerry and Morna had left earlier to visit someone they said lived nearby, but I was quite certain the closest thing they had to a neighbor was the castle itself. I suspected they'd left to allow us time to talk.

We sat across from each other in the living room. Eoin tried to busy himself with the television remote, randomly pushing the buttons, watching with fascination as the pictures changed on the screen. I sat silently for a few moments, knowing that my impatience was about to burst forth if he didn't set the remote down and start talking soon. Still, I knew my own fascination with the oddities of this century and so tried to be understanding.

"Eoin. Will ye please turn it off? It's time for ye to tell me why ye and Bri asked me to come here."

He didn't look at me immediately, instead staring at the remote as he searched for a way to stop the moving pictures. I reached over and pushed the red button, taking it from his hands as the television ceased its movement.

Rising up, he situated himself more comfortably on the couch and crossed his arms as he looked across at me. "Aye, I suppose 'tis time. I should tell ye beforehand that this wasna my idea. And I'm not too pleased with Bri for leaving me here to ask this of ye all alone. She knows more of this than I."

Why would Bri know more about anything than Eoin? She'd been living in my time for only a short period, and while I was still adjusting to the many differences of modern day life, I was sure she was still adjusting to the loss of modern conveniences. "Just get on with it, Eoin. I doona care which one of ye tells me. I'm only anxious to know. Ye have left me waiting for the past week."

"I know, and I'm sorry. I'm only unsure of how to explain this to ye." He cleared his throat, searching for a way to delay explanation even further.

"Eoin, if ye doona wish for me to cause ye physical harm, it would best serve ye to tell me right away." I leaned forward, placing my elbows on my knees and resting my head on my clenched fists, doing my best to look as threatening as possible.

"Bri seems to believe that ye were in love with Arran, and that is why ye left," he said, speaking quickly. "Ye dinna want to marry me, and ye couldna marry him, so ye decided to stay here. She believes that Arran is in love with ye, as well."

I stiffened, every muscle clenching as if to strangle me. My heart pounded painfully at the hope-filled words I'd stopped allowing myself to imagine I would ever hear. "Why?" I asked, breathless, my throat suddenly filled with cobwebs. "What reason would Bri have for believing such a thing?"

"Arran's behavior as of late. He has never been a stranger to the drink, but he has been drinking more than ever lately. And I havena seen him in the company of another woman in a long time. I do admit that he seems rather sad, but until Bri mentioned it, I dinna blame his demeanor on a broken heart."

It was hard for me to imagine Arran drinking more than he already did. The very day Arran had sent me away from him, he'd said he would soon share his bed with another. If he had not, perhaps Eoin was right. It filled me with a hope I could scarcely allow myself to believe without proof of his feelings.

"Has he told ye that he loves me, Eoin? Surely he would have told his own brother. Ye have always been his closest friend, and now that ye are married to Bri, what would have been the harm in him expressing his feelings to ye?" Rising, I moved restlessly about the room, the rush of mixed feelings making the space suddenly seem too small.

"No, lass, he hasna told me, but I think Bri may be right. There was something that happened shortly after our wedding that should have warned me of his feelings for ye."

I paused in front of the fireplace, keeping my back toward him, reluctant to allow him to see my eyes slowly filling with tears. "Aye? What happened?"

BETHANY CLAIRE

"There was a small fire set after the wedding that I was required to attend to, leaving Bri alone in our bedchamber. When I returned, I found Bri pinned to the wall in the hallway, with Arran kissing her madly."

I spun, my desire to hide my emotions suddenly forgotten. "What?"

"Aye, lass. I hit Arran, and he fell to the ground unconscious, and I threw Bri in the dungeon."

"Ye threw her in the dungeon, thinking she was me? On our wedding night!"

Eoin looked down at the floor. Someone else had clearly already reprimanded him for his actions. "I doona wish to talk about it. That is not the point."

"Aye, fine." I smiled at him briefly, urging him to continue.

"Arran blamed his actions on having too much to drink, but no man, no matter how drunk, would kiss a woman in such a familiar way unless he'd already done so many times before."

He quieted, and it was my turn to feel guilty. Regardless of how happy Eoin was with his new bride now, it was I who had been promised to him by my father, and I'd been unfaithful to him by the feelings I'd held for his brother.

"I'm sorry, Eoin. My behavior was disgraceful, and ye did nothing to deserve my betrayal of ye."

"Ach, think nothing of it, lass. Ye and I were not meant for a marriage together. All I want now is for my brother to be happy and for ye to find happiness, as well. If that is something the two of ye may find together, ye have my every blessing. If ye still love him, Blaire, we'd like ye to return home with us."

"Do ye truly believe he still loves me?" The words were already bubbling to the front of my mouth, but I wanted one more reassurance before agreeing to go home.

"Aye, I do. And Bri is certain of it. She's a wise woman. I've yet to find her wrong in anything."

I drew a deep breath, trying to calm my pounding heart. "Then, aye. I will come."

"Well done, Eoin."

Bri's voice in the doorway startled us both, and we stood to welcome her back.

"I knew you could convince her to come without me. Now, let's head to the castle. We've all been gone too long. Mom and Mary will both be in a tizzy."

---

1 646

*T*he wedding was arranged quickly. Only three days following his victory, Arran stood next to Edana in front of a crowd filled with his new clansmen. Eoin would certainly be surprised upon his arrival back home to find that his brother had moved away and was now a married laird. But Arran was sure Eoin would be happy to have the security of a guaranteed ally in the place of Ramsay.

Their ceremony was coming to a close, and while he repeated the words asked of him, in his imagination, each promise was made to the woman who owned his heart, not to the woman who stood beside him. As he closed his eyes to kiss his new bride, it was Blaire's face that he saw leaning into him.

CHAPTER 14

*T*ormod sat on a boulder perched atop the hillside cliff overlooking the ocean. As waves crashed upon the rocks, he scooted back in an effort to avoid the spray of water. It was a cold evening and the water was freezing; just another reason he was thankful he and his fellow clansmen did not live in such close proximity to the sea.

Edana was supposed to meet him here. She'd promised him right before the wedding ceremony that she would, but as the sun dropped lower and lower over the horizon, he began to question her loyalty to him.

While she'd spoken venomous words about Arran and his family, Tormod had seen Edana exchanging friendly conversation with Arran on more than one occasion. As the sun made its final bow against the horizon and night spread across the sky, Tormod stood. Just as he prepared to leave, he heard Edana's voice behind him.

"I'm sorry. I was delayed. What are we to do, Tormod? It will be difficult for us to meet now that I am married to Arran."

He couldn't have cared less about the tears she shed as she moved up beside him, burying her head in her hands. But if he was to maintain Edana's interest and loyalty, he knew he must show her sympathy.

"Come here, lass." He took her by the shoulders. "I doona wish to see ye cry. Yer marriage changes nothing. We shall be together as often as we can, and soon enough I will be laird."

Edana lifted her head. With great difficulty, Tormod kept his expression from revealing his displeasure at her red, tear-stained face.

"How can that be? The men love Arran. They are glad to have him as laird, and they willna take well to someone trying to take away his position."

"Nay, they willna just now," Tormod assured her. "In time, however, we shall find a way to change their opinion of him."

"How?" Again, Edana collapsed against him into a fit of sobs.

Tormod patted her back and stepped away, incapable of soothing the lass any further and weary of her weeping. "I doona know yet, but ye shall be spending much time with Arran from now on. Watch him, find something in his behavior that we can twist into an untruth, something it will be easy to convince others he is guilty of doing. It may take some time."

Edana looked up. Breathing deeply, as if trying to stop her tears, she said, "Aye, I shall do my best." She sniffed. "Tell me, Tormod, I need to know . . . I fear 'tis the only thing that shall get me through every horrible moment I must spend with Arran. Do ye love me? Would ye wish to be with me even if I would not make ye laird?"

He pulled her in close, wrapping his arms around her as he kissed her on the top of her head. "Aye, o'course I do. I love ye as much as I've ever loved anyone."

The second part of what he'd said was true, not that he'd ever loved anyone, save himself and perhaps his sister. The first, his declaration of love, was the lie, but it had slipped out easily. And perhaps he did love the lass a bit. At least, he loved what she would do for him and the power that would be delivered into his hands with her assistance.

Squeezing her once more in farewell, he eased her away and waved her off to the castle.

"Tis best that ye go. Yer new husband will be searching for ye, and we doona need to give him reason to be suspicious. I shall seek ye out after we have all arrived back home in a few weeks, after ye are both settled into yer castle."

"I shall miss ye every moment that I am not with ye, Tormod."

After she left him, he sat down on the rocks again, laughing quietly to himself. The lass was a fool to believe that he would care for her. He needed to find a way to destroy Arran soon. He didn't know how much more of the pathetic lass he could take.

---

*E*arly the next morning before the sun had risen, Arran snuck out of his room to retrieve his new bride from his late-mother's bedchamber. All castle workers and wedding guests, Mary being the one exception, assumed the newly married bride and groom had spent their first night of marriage together, and that was just the way he wanted to keep it. It wouldn't do if it was found out that neither of them had wanted to consummate their marriage.

After their wedding, Edana had briefly disappeared. When Arran finally found her, the marks of freshly cried tears stained her face. He'd rushed her off to his bedchamber to comfort her, but she'd pulled away, claiming her tears were caused by her fears of their wedding night.

While he suspected all new brides approached their wedding night with some anxiety, Edana's reaction seemed to be caused by more than just nerves. Arran had already suspected that Edana's father had harmed the lass in some way, but her apprehension for their wedding night only solidified his suspicions of just how monstrous Ramsay Kinnaird had been.

The lass's fears aside, Arran was not eager to consummate the marriage either, his feelings for her being only of a platonic nature. Instead, he'd not questioned her, not pushed the ritual they were both expected to complete, but ushered her quietly down the hall to the safety of her own room.

Arran knew the consummation would have to be completed, but that could come in time, when the bonds of friendship were a little stronger between the two of them. For now, he would simply collect her from her room, and together they would make their way to the stables where they would meet with his new clansmen and begin their journey to the new Conall Castle.

---

*A*delle cast Mary a puzzled frown. "What do you mean they didn't consummate their marriage? How on earth would you know that, Mary? Goodness, I know you're nosy, but I didn't know you were a peeping Tom. What did you do, cut a peep hole into Arran's bedroom?" She laughed at her own wit.

Mary had to refrain from whopping the woman on the nose. Bri, she loved, but it was going to take more time to adjust to the loud-mouthed, say-anything ways of her mother. "I doona know what a 'peeping Tom' is, but I doona believe I like what ye are suggesting. O'course I dinna spy on them. I know they dinna consummate the marriage because Arran had me prepare his mother's room for Edana to stay in. They dinna spend the night together." Mary continued kneading the dough as her nosy kitchen visitor sat across from her, watching.

"No! Why? It's because Bri was right, isn't it? He does still love Blaire. I knew we should've stopped that marriage, Mary!

Perhaps, it's not too late to do something. If they've not consummated it, it's not actually binding, is it?"

"I doona know why they dinna spend the night together, but aye, I do believe Bri was right. But it doesna matter, there is nothing we can do because everyone else believes the marriage is consummated, and we are not going to tell them anything different. Do ye understand me?"

"Why? We must. Bri is going to kill us both when she gets back here with Blaire, and we've let Arran run off and marry somebody else."

Mary threw her hands up in exasperation, sending a cloud of flour soaring into the air. "What do ye think she would have expected us to do to stop him? Arran listens to no one, especially when it is someone trying to stop him from doing something foolish. If Blaire returns, which I doona think she will, she will overcome it in time. I doona like it for either of them, but both have made their own choices. 'Tis not our place to meddle."

"Not our place? That's what mothers do, Mary. And regardless of your position here in the castle, you know as well as I do that you are just as much a mother to those lads as their real mother was. They were young when they lost her, and you've been there for them and loved them since they were babes."

Mary couldn't help but smile. Adelle was right; she loved Eoin and Arran as if they were her own.

Movement in the doorway caused her to glance up from the heap of dough. Kip approached her, carrying a letter. Mary turned to dip her hands into a bucket of water to cleanse them of the flour.

"What is it?" she asked, shaking her hands dry. She reached for the parchment in her husband's hand.

"I doona know. Saw a lad riding up to deliver it, so I stopped him and told him I'd take it here myself. It's addressed to Eoin.

Seeing as both lads are gone, I expect that 'tis ye that should open it."

"Aye, o'course." Mary broke the seal and unfolded the parchment. She shook her head as she read the words. "It wouldna do for Old Mary to have one day of rest. One day with both of the lads gone for me to pretend that I live a life of leisure. Nay, such a small wish is too much for me to receive." She paused and pointed at her husband. "Kip, ye will need to gather every one near us to help get the castle in order. We doona only have to clean up the mess our guests left us, but we have a new batch of visitors arriving. Lady McMillan and her three sons will be here the day after next."

CHAPTER 15

he Castle Formerly Known As Kinnaird

The first evening Edana spent at what was now considered Conall Castle but was once Kinnaird Castle, she felt her father's presence everywhere. The remains of his hatred, his abuse, his insanity weighed upon her, taunting her, pleading with her to finish what he'd started.

Her father had given his life to defeat the Conalls, and it had all been for nothing. His worst nightmare had come true. A Conall now led, and his only daughter was now married to one, as well.

Edana moved through the hallways haunted by the memories of her childhood, a childhood filled with fear, filled with manipulation, filled with abuse. Now that her father was gone, she wanted to move on, to live a happier life than the one he had provided for her. But with her father's plan for the Conalls' demise unfinished, she knew his presence would remain over her, tempting her to the madness that he'd surrendered to. The only hope she had of finding peace and ending his control on her life, was to finish what he'd begun.

The Conalls were too confident, too powerful, and too trusting for their own good. Those reasons alone would have been enough to make her hate them, but their defeat of her father had chained her to him. Until she was released from his hold, she would never be able to find the happiness she knew was possible for her with Tormod by her side.

Arran had already retired for the evening in her father's old room. While he'd given her permission to spend the night elsewhere, Edana knew it was best not to put off the inevitable. The marriage had to be consummated or be considered invalid. She knew the servants of this castle well enough to know that they would speak if she did not visit her husband's room.

She couldn't allow questions to arise about the marriage. She needed to do as Tormod had bid her, to spend time with Arran and find a weakness they could exploit to his demise.

Edana paced back and forth, pausing in front of Arran's door with each passing. She was certain that what must follow would be some of the worst moments of her life. Thinking of it brought back flashes of horror from her past that she did her best to push away. This would be different than the times before. She was older. No longer a child. And she was now choosing this of her own free will.

Tormod had yet to touch her beyond a swift kiss during their stolen moments together. Still, she knew the scars of her past would have caused her to be just as frightened as she was now if it were he she must bed tonight, rather than a man she didn't love.

She hoped Arran wouldn't notice the lack of blood. It could mean the end of their marriage if he did. For many men it would, but she suspected Arran would be different. Just another reason he could be easily defeated. He was caring and kind, and that made him weak.

Gathering her courage, she glanced at her reflection in a piece of armory hanging on the wall. Pushing her hair out of her face, she pinched her cheeks to bring up a blush. Before she could change her mind, Edana knocked on her husband's door.

***

*T*he dark castle lacked access to sunlight, unlike Arran's childhood home that was filled with such great light. It wasn't only the structure's positioning in relation to the sunrise and sunset that made this castle dark; the scarred remnants of Ramsay's legacy were etched deep into every piece of furniture and tapestry. Arran wouldn't allow that to be the case for long.

He planned to turn the castle into a place of happiness, a place his children would enjoy for many, many years. A place where his new clansmen could rest assured that they were now represented by a fair and just leader rather than the abomination who'd ruled over them before.

He'd been in his bedchamber for hours, composing a letter to send to his brother, hoping to provide Eoin with more explanation on his surprising choices as of late. He had just finished the letter and was preparing to retire when he heard a soft knock on the door.

Glancing down at himself, a new habit he'd formed thanks to Mary, and finding himself decently clothed, he went to greet his visitor.

Edana stood before him, draped in her nightgown, hair down and pushed back behind her ears. She held a candle which shook lightly in her hands, a sure sign of her nerves, and Arran knew instantly why she'd come to him.

He invited her in, but his insides twisted. He was sure his former self, the Arran before Blaire, would think him mad, but he still found himself rather uneager to bed his new wife.

Despite his misgivings, it would be impossible for him to deny her. He knew what courage it took for her to come to him, and it was an act that must be performed. It was the only way to secure his place as laird, to legitimize their marriage, and he knew that Edana was offering him a kindness by recognizing that fact and offering herself to him without his bidding.

But there was no need to hurry into the act right away. He suspected that she would be much like a frightened animal. If he wished her not to bolt, he would need to take his time and move gently.

He walked to a table near the doorway and poured her some wine, extending it in her direction as he moved to stand away from her, leaning his back against the wall.

"How are ye this evening, Edana? I am surprised to find ye here so late. Is there something the matter with your room?" He needed to be certain he was right about her reasons for coming to see him.

She downed the wine quickly, and Arran couldn't keep his eyes from widening in surprise.

"All is fine with my room. 'Tis the same as it has always been."

She extended the cup back to him, and he quickly refilled it before resuming his place against the wall. "Ye know that ye are welcome in here, Edana, but might I ask - is there a particular reason for yer visit?"

She set her wine down and moved toward him. He tensed all over, unsure of how to proceed. She leaned into him, gently kissing him on the cheek and whispered softly as her lips lingered near his mouth. "I think ye know, Arran. I'm no longer afraid of ye."

She kissed him then, softly, slowly, doing her best to seduce him, but he could feel the soft tremble in her lips. Gently lacing his fingers with hers, he pulled away from her.

"I doona believe ye, lass. I can tell ye are frightened by the way ye are shaking, but that is fine. 'Tis not an uncommon thing for a woman to be quite scared when she is unaccustomed to sharing her bed with a man. But ye do know that this is something we must do, aye? Tis why ye have come." She looked up at him, her eyes hesitant, and his sympathy for her made his heart ache.

"Aye. Ye are now my husband, and 'tis yer right to have me. It would be improper for me to deny ye."

He brought his right hand up to her face, cupping her cheek gently as he tried to reassure her with his eyes. "Nay, lass. 'Tis not my right, but it shall be my pleasure, and I am honored that ye offer me the gift of yerself. Please know that I would never hurt ye, lass, and I will never do anything ye doona want me to. Doona ever be afraid to tell me no. Ye doona belong to me, lass. Ye belong to none but yerself. Doona ever forget that or let anyone make ye believe differently."

Arran pulled her in close so that he could place his mouth to hers. He slowly warmed her lips with soft, feather-light kisses. He wanted it to be her choice, something she wanted of him. It would be difficult enough for him to be the lover to her that she deserved with the image of Blaire burned forever in his heart, but he feared the task would be impossible if he knew Edana offered herself to him out of duty.

As he continued to press gently against her lips, her mouth gradually opened to him, matching his rhythm as he increased the intensity of the kiss.

Accepting her invitation, Arran pulled back and turned to put out the fire and candles.

CHAPTER 16

*A*delle rushed frantically around the castle, ensuring that each job placed on Mary's task list was completed perfectly. She knew as well as anyone that Conall Castle was Mary's ship to run, but with the quick succession of guests leaving and new visitors arriving today, the mess around the castle was more than even the great Mary could accomplish on her own.

Adelle knew that she gave the old, uptight drill sergeant a hard time. Truth was, the woman simply amazed her. Adelle suspected that despite the older woman's crusty exterior, Mary was pretty fond of her, as well. Seeing the stress that the news of their arriving-any-minute guests had brought to the other woman, Adelle wanted to do all she could to help her new friend.

Satisfied that the castle sparkled enough for even the most discerning eyes, she followed her nose to the kitchen where the salty smell of stew caused her stomach to growl.

She'd expected to find Mary bent over a large pot, stirring and seasoning away until whatever concoction she'd worked up for the evening meal was to her satisfaction, but instead she found the kitchen unmanned. The room was completely empty save for the loaves of bread laid out and the bubbling, steaming, saliva-building stew warming over the fire. It was all too much for Adelle's over-eager stomach to take. With a quick glance around the area to confirm that she truly was alone, Adelle tip-toed into the kitchen.

She was doing Mary a favor by attending to the food herself. Who knew what sort of contaminants or poisons could have been slipped into the pot while Mary was away? The only proper thing to do was to test it herself, to make sure that it was safe for the consumption of their guests.

Reaching up toward one of the room's many shelves, Adelle grabbed a wooden bowl that she swiftly dipped into the steaming stew, filling it to the brim with yummy goodness.

She seated herself with her back to the doorway. She didn't want to get caught red-handed if someone decided to come down into the kitchen. She glanced around for a utensil to eat her stolen prize. Finding nothing, she quickly brushed her fingertips on the hem of her dress and, judging them clean enough for the time being, dipped her fingers inside to pick up a juicy slab of meat.

Mary had outdone herself with this one. Each bite seemed more delicious than the last, and Adelle lost herself as she ravenously chowed down on Mary's creation. She would forever be grateful for the rapid metabolism she'd inherited from her own mother. Without it, Adelle knew without doubt that she would weigh three hundred pounds as opposed to her slight, size two frame.

When she heard voices coming from the floor above her, she stopped her prize-winning chow-down. Straining to listen, she heard Mary's voice welcoming the guests. Knowing her appearance would be quickly expected, Adelle swallowed the last piece of meat whole and raised the bowl to her mouth, tipping it high so that she could drink the last of the stew.

Adelle shoved the bowl back onto the shelf, telling herself she would do her best to remember to come back and clean it. She took the stairs two at a time, hoping she would be able to greet their new guests before Mary showed them to their rooms.

When she made it to the top of the stairs, she paused quickly to catch her breath. Finally, moving with as much grace as she could muster, she stepped into the main entranceway to greet their guests.

"*W*hat did I tell ye about getting into the kitchen when I'm not in there? No one eats before mealtime." Mary ground out the words to Adelle between clenched teeth as soon as they'd seen their guests to their rooms and they began making their way down to the kitchen together.

Adelle's eyes widened as she turned to glance guiltily at Mary. "I have no idea what you are talking about."

"Aye, ye do. Doona lie to me. Look!" Mary moved in front of her, effectively blocking Adelle from taking another step down the small staircase. Taking her by surprise, she reached up and brushed a finger on either side of Adelle's mouth, pulling her hand away to reveal light brown globs of stew.

Adelle sat down on the step behind her and threw her forehead into the palm of her hand.

"Oh, no. Please don't tell me. I didn't spend all that time visiting with Lady McMillan and her sons with that goopy mess all over my face, did I?"

Mary chuckled loudly, obviously pleased with herself as Adelle continued to sink further into a state of mortification.

"Aye, ye did. I canna believe ye dinna notice them staring at yer mouth. I think poor Baodan almost wiped it for ye more than once, but he never worked up the nerve." Mary collapsed into hearty laughter again.

Adelle stood and stormed off, continuing to make her own way down the stairs. "Why didn't you tell me?" she called back to the other woman. "I don't think I've ever been this embarrassed in my entire life."

"Why dinna I tell ye? Because that's what ye deserve for sticking yer mouth in things that ye know ye are not meant to. And as wild as ye are, 'tis certain ye have embarrassed yerself far worse than this before."

"That is completely and totally beside the point." Adelle reached the kitchen first, and before Mary could protest, retrieved her used bowl and filled it up with stew once more. "And don't you say a word about me getting another bowl."

Mary smiled, then broke into laughter. "Aye, go ahead and eat all ye like, Adelle. Why, the look on their faces. Well, I havena enjoyed myself so much in quite a long time. Yer foolishness has brought me great joy. I no longer care what ye eat."

 *resent Day*

"*Y*e look a fair mess, Eoin. Do ye think we could have Morna take a photo of ye in that outfit that we could take back with us? I think it would provide much entertainment." I smiled as Eoin, moving uncomfortably in the restraint of his denim jeans, rewarded me with a quick but vicious glare.

"Ye are a cruel woman, Blaire," he said.

Bri had been wary of taking him back to the spell room

dressed in his usual attire. While Eoin was far too tall to fit into any of Jerry's clothes, Morna had been able to come up with a pair of jeans, tennis shoes, and a dark blue sweater that fit Eoin perfectly. I suspected casting up clothes was a simple task compared to making it possible for people to travel through time.

Morna turned to address all of us as we gathered in the entranceway of her home, preparing to make our exit back to the past. "I shall miss ye all dearly, but remember that ye can find me if ye need to, aye?"

We nodded in unison, and Bri stepped forward to squeeze Morna's neck. "Thank you. And you'll help Mitsy if she needs it, right? You remember what she looks like, don't you?"

Morna hugged her tightly and gave her a comforting pat on the back. "Aye, o'course we do. And the inn will always be available to yer friend to find if she needs it. The spell room, as well. Now, ye best all be on yer way so that ye can sneak into the room before they lock the castle up for the evening."

Bri had remained unusually quiet since she'd arrived from her trip and, after the exchange I'd just overheard between her and Morna, I suspected it had something to do with Mitsy. I would have to remember to ask her about it once we were home and things were settled.

We each said our goodbyes and, within the hour, found ourselves in the spell room once more. The spell was easily cast, and we clung to one another as the all-too-familiar pain ripped through us and we all disappeared into dust.

CHAPTER 17

1 646

*O*ur re-entry into the past brought with it the expected headache and a short moment of confusion. It took me a little longer than Eoin and Bri to recover from the travel. They adjusted almost immediately back to their usual selves.

Eoin scowled at his wife. "I doona care how much ye like the way my bum looks in jeans, I willna wear them again. As soon as I can pry them off me, I shall burn them until every last scrap has disappeared."

"Don't you dare!" Bri exclaimed. "You don't have to wear them all the time, but for God's sake, don't burn them! That's the only set of modern male clothing we have. What if somebody else ever needs to go forward again?"

"We are all here now. I doona have any plans of going forward ever again."

Bri returned Eoin's scowl. "Neither do I, but seriously, quit being such a child. You're not going to burn them. Just take them off. I'm folding them up and storing them with our clothing."

With my vision clear again and my headache slowly receding, I slipped into a dark corner of the room to change my clothes in privacy. "She is right, Eoin," I called out to them. "I doona know why ye would want to burn them. I would love to stay in my jeans forever. I doona wish to go back to wearing my old clothes at all."

Bri smiled at me as she extended a dress for me to slip on in place of my modern clothes. "Don't worry. You can still wear them some. Sometimes I sneak down here just to put them on. If we can ever get Eoin and Arran to leave us alone in the castle, we will put them on and just strut around all day and shock the bejeezus out of every person we see. It will be great fun!"

I laughed, twisting to the side so that Bri could help me with the laces. "Aye, I look forward to the day. I hope my hair grows fast. Being back here, it suddenly feels too short."

"Doona worry about that, lass," said Eoin. "'Tis not that short, but as to the clothing, ye both would be fools to do such a thing. If the wrong people were to see ye dressed in such a way, they'd have ye burnt for witchcraft, and they wouldna all together be lying. Now, let's go and make our return known." Eoin turned and left, leaving Bri and me alone in the small spell room.

Bri turned to follow her husband, but I reached out to stop her, placing a hand on her arm. "Bri, do ye think Arran will be pleased that I am here? I'm quite nervous to see him." She reached up and squeezed my hand.

"I really think he will be. Don't be nervous. We will look for Mary and my mother first. I don't expect Arran will be in the castle, anyhow. He spends most of his time either in the stables with Kip or drinking in the village."

Taking a deep breath, I followed her out of the spell room.

Nerves were senseless. I knew they would do nothing to change the outcome of whatever reunion was about to occur.

*T*he room grew warm as Eoin, Bri, Adelle, Mary, and I sat surrounding the work table in Mary's kitchen. That's where we'd found Adelle and Mary, and the excitement of their welcome had quickly become a muddled chaos as everyone seemed to speak at once.

Eventually we'd sat together, each person eager to hear a different set of news. I feigned attention for most of the time as I anxiously awaited the answer to the one question I was too afraid to ask.

When Mary finally said it aloud, my entire body went numb.

"He isna here, Eoin. All of Kinnaird's clansmen have left, and his former territory shall now be known as a Conall territory, as well." She cast me a wary glance. "Arran is laird there now. He has married Edana."

I felt as if a thousand pins pricked my skin at Mary's response, and my heart sank to the pit of my stomach.

"What?" Bri's voice was shrill and panicked as she glanced my way.

Mary cast her eyes downward. "Aye. I'm afraid 'tis true. They left here only a few nights ago."

I could tell she was not pleased by the news she had to share with us. I was helpless in discerning my own feelings, the excited hope and bright future I'd been imagining suddenly dying like the candle flame I found myself staring into. At least Arran wasn't here to tell me the news himself. The words from his mouth would have felt like rejection all over again. Perhaps now I could simply leave, return home to my father whom I was sure would be more than happy to marry me off to another man of his choosing.

"Why didn't you stop him?" Bri snapped at her mother.

"There was nothing we could do, Bri. You made us swear not to tell him where'd you actually gone. We couldn't give him a good reason not to marry her without telling him what the two of you were up to."

"I don't care. That was the one reason good enough to break your promise." Bri looked to be on the brink of tears.

Wanting to stop her from blaming her mother any further, I let the one question at the forefront of my own mind slip out. "Does he love her?"

Silence rewarded my question. Adelle and Mary exchanged knowing glances, both obviously unsure if they should give me an answer.

"No." Bri answered for them. And Mary and Adelle nodded in agreement.

For some reason, both women apparently thought that it would be even more devastating for me to learn that Arran had married Edana if he was not in love with her. And perhaps it was.

For if Arran had married for love, I would have been left with no choice but to move on with my life. To grow old, certain in the knowledge that there had never been any hope that I might spend my life at his side.

But knowing that he didn't love her would make healing and moving on more difficult. I would live every day wondering, hoping and wishing that he was thinking of me, wanting me by his side instead of Edana. I would live every day imagining what my life could have been like if his marriage had only been delayed by a few days.

Mary cleared her throat. "Yer Aunt Kenna arrived yesterday, Eoin. Baodan, Eoghanan, and Niall, as well. I am unsure of the reason for their visit, but I think 'tis time for ye to go and greet them, let them know that ye are back."

Eoin stood and nodded. "Aye, o'course. I suspect they've come to pay their condolences about Father. They were in the midst of their own grief when he died. I should have reached out to them myself."

Bri reached for his hand. "I'll let you visit with them a moment. I'll come up shortly. I want a chance to visit with Blaire alone." Bri dropped his hand and turned to her mother and Mary, sending them an unmistakable message with her eyes. Understanding, they stood and followed Eoin out of the kitchen.

I rose and moved to the seat across from Bri, silently looking down at the table as I waited for her to speak.

"I'm so sorry. I'm so very, very sorry, Blaire," she said after a time. "When we left, there was not the least bit of talk of Arran and Edana marrying. I scarcely saw the two of them together, and he never flirted with her. I never would've come to get you if I'd known."

I wasn't angry with her. Of course she wouldn't have known, and Eoin certainly wouldn't have asked me to return if he'd had any idea. "Ye doona need to apologize to me, Bri. I know that ye dinna know."

"If you want to go back, I'll go one more time so you don't have to do it alone. I'll help you get set up wherever you like. I can stay with you, teach you some things, get you a good job. I'll even have all of my bank accounts transferred to you. Whatever you'd like."

"I doona wanna go back, Bri." I looked up at her as she stood, sensing she had more to say and that I wasna going to like whatever it was.

"I was hoping you would say that. We're going to go pay Arran a visit. You and me. We're leaving in the morning."

I shook my head as forcefully as I could. "I will do no such thing, Bri. Are ye mad? What good would that bring?"

"I don't know, exactly. But I do know that you have to see him. You'll wonder forever about him, if you don't. You'll wonder if he still cares, or even if you cared for him as much as you'd thought. If anything, perhaps seeing him one last time will bring you closure."

I'd only known Bri a few weeks, but I could recognize enough of her mother in her to know that arguing would not change her mind. "Is this not my decision to make?"

She smiled and shook her head. "No. Not at all. And don't tell Eoin. He'll only try to stop us from leaving. Meet me at the stables at dawn."

She exited the kitchen before I could respond, and I was left to ponder through a sleepless night just what new humiliation and heartbreak would await me at Arran's new home.

CHAPTER 18

*E*arly the next morning, with dawn still some time away from peeking through the night's blackness, I heard a knock on the bedchamber door.

Still wide awake, I answered quickly to see Bri with a small bag draped over her shoulders. She couldn't have looked any more excited.

"Come on, let's go! I told Mary of our plan last night so that she could have Kip ready some horses. Don't worry. She promised she wouldn't tell Eoin. I think she's trying to make amends for letting Arran get married."

I shook my head in disagreement. "She has nothing to make amends for. Arran isna a man that is easily kept from doing what he wishes."

Bri's smile briefly disappeared as she stepped into the room to help me gather a few things for the journey. "You're right. I shouldn't have been so harsh with Mary and my mother. I owe them both an apology. And I'll give them one just as soon as we get back, but right now, we need to go before Eoin rolls over and realizes I've gone."

"Doona ye think he will be furious when he finds out? Do ye not think he will come after us?"

Bri's smile returned, and I found that I was changing my opinion of her. I'd first thought her to be a rather serious-mannered, laced-tight kind of person, but upon spending further time with her, I was learning that she was more mischievous than she let others know. "Well, normally I believe he would come after us immediately. But there are guests here now, and I don't think he will leave them. He'll be spit-fire angry, but he'll get over it."

"Aye, well he's not my husband. If ye are certain we should go, I willna worry myself over it." I picked up the bag Bri had filled. Moving as silently as we could through the corridors of the castle, we made our way out the back door.

A torch burned outside the stable entrance. As we approached, Bri called out, "Kip, are the horses ready?"

"Aye!" came Mary's response from inside, surprising us both. "I already sent Kip back to bed, but they are all ready for us to leave."

Bri and I exchanged a questioning look. "Mary, what are you doing?" Bri asked as we hurried inside. I stood back, trying not to laugh at the sight of the short, round woman balancing astride a horse, beaming the brightest smile I'd ever seen.

"What does it look like I'm doing? I'm coming with ye. I've been telling Eoin and Arran for years that I needed a break. After the past few weeks, I feel I've earned it. Besides, I need to see with my own eyes how Arran is faring in his new home." She nudged the horse with her pudgy heels, and it took off at a slow trot out of the stable.

Neither Bri or I argued. After mounting our horses, we followed Mary. And away from Conall Castle the three of us went.

*I*t turned out that Bri was perhaps a tad less adventurous than she wanted to be. By midday, she'd worried herself into such a state of guilt that she rode in complete silence, offering only her pained expression to keep us company.

I, on the other hand, enjoyed every minute of being astride a horse again. The feeling of being out of the city without the car horns and other modern-day noises that had kept me consistently nervous had me feeling more like myself than I had in ages. As long as I tried to keep our journey's final destination out of my mind, I found myself even feeling happy.

Mary remained cheerful but consistently complained about the torture her backside was experiencing from riding atop a horse for such a long time. My own backside was feeling the effects, as well. The months I'd spent away had softened my previously horse-accustomed bum.

As the day progressed, Mary's good humor found a way to crack Bri's worry-creased brow, and the mood lightened. By the time we drew our horses up at the side of a small break in the trees to camp for the evening, all of our middles ached from laughter.

We dismounted, our bodies stiff and achy, and slowly hobbled along to make camp. Each of us moved as if decades older than our given ages. I started a fire while Mary lay out the bread and cheese she'd packed for the journey. Bri went in the direction of a nearby stream to gather some water. Shortly thereafter, we each lay under the stars, our stomachs full and our bodies sore.

I was on the edge of sleep, and I expected Bri was, as well, due to the loud snort that burst forth from her, when Mary's loud, overly-excited voice caused us both to sit straight up.

"What is it, Mary? Did something frighten ye?" I scooted

closer to the fire so that I could see the expression on her face more clearly. She looked more excited than anyone should have been after riding for hours and sleeping on the ground.

"Aye, me bum was so sore I almost forgot what I took from Arran's old room. Wake yerselves up, lassies. I have just the thing to soothe our aching bodies."

Bri, who was sitting up but hunched over in a half-asleep position, looked up at Mary from under heavy eyelids. "Sleep? Yes, I believe sleep will do the trick just fine."

"Nay, 'tisna sleep, though I expect we shall all sleep quite soundly after we partake of what I've brought for us. Now wake yerself up." Mary stood and made her way over to her bag, which was propped against a nearby tree. Reaching inside, she withdrew a large bottle of something undoubtedly stronger than wine.

"Mary!" Bri's shocked voice echoed through the open space around us, sending the maid into a fit of giggles.

"I told ye I was in need of a break from my work and a break is what I shall have. I doona think there is anything wrong with Old Mary allowing herself just one night to be foolish. Now, ye lasses will join me whether ye like to or not." She extended two wooden cups to us and we took them without protest.

Once they were filled, we all sipped silently, our exhaustion making us far less enjoyable company than Mary seemed to desire. Eventually, I could take no more of Mary's disappointed glares and turned to address Bri.

"Do ye know of any games? I couldna make sense of most of them, but when I was serving drinks in Edinburgh, people would at times play games while they were drinking."

"Well, I'll confess to my lack of drinking knowledge. Teaching gave me little time for a social life, but I suppose I know of one or two games we could play, if Mary still wishes to continue her wild night."

Mary nodded, smiling widely as she poured more liquor into her cup. "Aye, o'course I do. Have ye yet to see my change me mind about something once it has been set?"

---

*S*hortly thereafter, Bri and I found ourselves tending to a very rambunctious Mary. Twice, she had thought it would be a grand idea for us to take off our clothes and run naked through the break in the trees where we'd set up camp.

Each time, we'd quickly diverted her attention elsewhere.

The game *Never Have I Ever*, as described by Bri, had started off innocently enough. We'd given Mary the opportunity to ask questions first. In her effort to get both of us drunk, she'd asked questions that she knew would require us to take a drink, such as, "Never have I ever travelled through time." But soon the questions were turned over to Bri and me. It seemed no matter how wild our inquiry, Mary had participated in the activity. Soon, I'd learned things about Mary that not only shocked me but made me slightly nervous to be in her company. It was certain neither of us would ever look at the woman in quite the same way again.

Thank goodness, what seemed to be a never-ending bottle of whiskey finally ran dry. Shortly after, an exhausted and bleary-eyed Mary succumbed to sleep.

CHAPTER 19

Before sunrise, I rose to gather water. The trip didn't take long, and while I'd expected to find both Mary and Bri still asleep when I returned, Mary was fully awake and busily ordering Bri to get up and help her pack up camp. Mary showed no signs of suffering after her bountiful whiskey consumption, instead seeming rather more rested than either Bri or me.

"How do ye feel, Mary? I was sure that ye'd sleep for quite a while longer." I bent to roll up my belongings, following Mary so that we could strap them to our horses.

"I doona know why ye would ask such a question. I feel fine, o'course."

She wouldn't look at me, keeping her head down as we gathered another load to bring back to the horses. Bri joined us, and having heard the beginning of our conversation, joined in. "How could you possibly feel fine, Mary? You drank more in the course of an evening than Arran drinks in a day. Do you even remember anything about last night?"

Mary stopped walking and whirled on both of us, quickly setting down her load. "Nay, I doona, and it doesna matter. Both of ye are never to mention what happened last night ever again. Do ye understand? I've never behaved in such a way, and I find myself feeling a wee bit ashamed this morning."

I shook my head. "Doona feel that way. There's no need."

Bri nodded. "Yes, please don't feel that way, Mary. You've been under a lot of stress with Eoin and me being gone, Arran leaving, and then the visitors. Not to mention, my mother."

Mary smiled, seeming to forgive herself a little. "Aye. We shall blame it on yer mother. Now, let's finish gathering camp and be on our way. I doona wish to spend another night on the ground. I believe that neither of ye will speak of this, not that anyone would believe ye even if ye did."

She was right. No one would. Laughing, we packed up, then Bri and I hoisted Mary's short legs up onto her horse. After we mounted our own beasts, we moved on in the direction of the new Conall Castle. I tried to keep my mind on anything other than the knowledge that I would be seeing Arran again – and meeting his new wife – come nightfall.

The Castle Formerly Known as Kinnaird

"Did we know that visitors were arriving?" Arran followed the messenger to the entranceway of the castle, all the while wondering if his new guests were just one more thing he'd forgotten. The many duties required by the laird were far more than he'd realized, and each day he found himself more impressed with the way his brother had handled the responsibilities back home so soon after their father's death.

"Nay, sir. Ye would have been informed if we had received news of their arrival beforehand. 'Tis three women, sir."

Arran stopped before opening the castle's main doors and faced the messenger. "Three women? Do ye know who they are?"

"They say they are from yer old home, sir. An old lady and two women who look like the same person, but they doona talk the same. One of them talks verra strangely."

Arran clasped the man on the shoulder more in an effort to steady himself than to gain attention. It couldn't be true. Blaire was gone, that painful ache in his chest a reminder of her absence every day. "Ye must be mistaken. 'Tis only two women, aye?"

"I'm not mistaken. There are three. The first two insisted I let them in right away, but I told them I wouldna do so until I spoke to ye. The third woman was verra quiet. I noticed her for that reason. See for yerself."

The man pulled the large doors open, giving Arran no time to prepare himself for what he both hoped and dreaded he would find. He found Blaire's eyes right away—the pain, passion, and yearning there, a sure reflection of what she saw in his own.

He wanted to run to her, to gather her in his arms and tell her he was sorry for sending her away, sorry that he hadn't denied his brother and married her when he'd had the chance. He almost did just that, but was stopped by a slight touch on his back.

He jerked away involuntarily, and he looked to his side to find Edana standing there.

"I dinna know that Donal had two daughters. They look remarkably similar. Are ye not going to show them inside? They're family, aye?"

"Aye, o'course I am. Would ye go inside and have our table readied for three more? I shall escort them in at once." Edana nodded and turned from him, and he silently chided himself for briefly forgetting the existence of his new wife.

Bri dismounted her horse quickly and came over to him,

throwing her arms around his neck and smacking him lightly on the back of his head.

"It's good to see you, but you are a damn fool, Arran." Whispering in his ear, she added, "How could you go and do such a stupid, stupid thing?" When he pulled back to explain, Bri quieted him by pulling him in close again. "Don't you dare try to explain it to me right now. We can talk about it after we eat. Go and squeeze Mary. She's been missing you like crazy. And don't say a word to Blaire right now. You can't upset her before she is forced to sit with Edana. You can speak with her later."

She finally loosened her grip, and Arran stepped away. Quietly, he murmured, "I doona understand. How is Blaire here? Why?" Questions coursed through his mind, questions he knew would have to go unanswered for the moment. "What will we tell Edana? She doesna know about the spell room. No one does."

Bri smiled at him reassuringly, but it did nothing to soothe his uneasy mind. "Don't worry, I'll think of something to tell her over dinner. We need to come up with a story, anyway. We will have to tell it a lot. No one has seen the both of us together yet. Now, go to Mary and help her down from her horse, then see her inside. Blaire and I will find our way shortly."

Arran nodded and walked toward Mary. After helping her slide off of her horse, he yanked her into a large embrace. He kissed her soundly on the cheek before rearing back at the smell that rose around them. "Ye smell like an ale house, Mary. Did ye bathe in a basin of whiskey?"

The old woman flailed in his arms, and her face reddened as she smacked him hard on the arm. He seemed to be having that effect on the Conall women this evening. Both Mary and Bri had hit him since their arrival.

"What do ye mean by that? Do ye not know me well enough to believe that I would do such a thing? Why, ye are most likely smelling yerself!"

Arran laughed and stepped away from her. "Aye, I'm sure ye are right, Mary. Now let me show ye inside to yer room where ye shall rest as long as ye are here. Ye work hard enough at home. I want ye to do naught but breathe for a while."

She laughed, and Arran pulled her in close again. Then, doing his best to avoid Blaire's gaze, he looked down while showing Mary inside.

A knock on the bedchamber door caused my breath to lodge in my throat, but upon hearing Bri's voice on the other side, I released a sigh of relief. I swung the door open to be greeted with the hefty smell of meat and wine as Bri carried my dinner inside.

"Here you go. It was difficult for me to explain why I needed to bring you food when supposedly you were too ill to go to dinner. I'm sure Arran knew I was lying."

I sat quickly, shoveling the delicious meal into my mouth as it eased my grumbling stomach. "I shouldna have come here. It was wrong of me to do so. Did ye not see the way Edana looked at him when she came outside?"

Bri crossed her arms as she stared down at me. "No. I didn't. I was too busy looking at how Arran couldn't take his eyes off you."

"He dinna even speak to me." I quickly finished off the food and stood, moving to the door. "I canna stay here, Bri. I'm going back tonight."

I made to open the door but was stopped by Bri's tight grip on my arm. "Ok, if you want to go, that's fine. We will leave tomorrow, but you can't go anywhere tonight. You don't know the way back by yourself anyhow. I'm sorry. It was wrong of me to make you come here."

I could see the sense in her words. It would be foolish for me to travel at night all alone, but I knew that I couldn't spend another moment inside the castle. "Doona be sorry. Ye have no reason to be so. Ye are right. I willna leave, but I need to get outside of the castle. I dinna know seeing him would upset me so. I'll be brushing the horses in the stables."

I shut the door before Bri had a chance to speak.

CHAPTER 20

*A*rran knocked lightly on the door, hoping that Bri would open it quickly before Edana saw him sneaking into the room of their female guests. She'd been away in her own bedchamber for some time, but he knew her to be a nighttime wanderer. She was finding her way into his bed much more frequently.

Blaire's absence at dinner had surprised him. He knew she wasn't ill, not that he could blame her for not wanting to see him. She must think he truly didn't care for her, to be able to marry so soon after what they had shared together. If only Blaire knew how she occupied his every thought, pained his every breath when he wasn't near her.

"Come in. Did you not hear me calling you through the door, telling you that you could enter?"

He'd lost himself in his own thoughts of regret and self-pity, forgetting that he was standing outside the door until he heard Bri's voice in front of him. He looked up, pulling himself out of his trance as he stepped inside. "Nay, I dinna. I was thinking."

"I'm sure you were. What did you think about what I told

Edana about Blaire and me? Do you think she bought it? Will everybody else?"

Arran frowned as he tried to remember what story Bri had told. It was the last thing on his mind. All he could think about was Blaire. "Forgive me, I doona know what ye told her. I am not feeling like myself."

Bri reached out to lay a hand on his back, and he smiled, knowing she understood.

"I know. I'm sorry. We can talk about it later. She's not here, Arran. She said she was going to the stables."

He nodded, briefly shutting his eyes as he pictured her there, slender fingers running gently down whatever horse was lucky enough to share her company. "O'course she is. The lass loves horses as much as I do. She willna want to see me, though. Why is she here, Bri? How did she get back to this time?"

"Eoin and I went for her. That's where we were, not at Bran's."

Arran had suspected as much. Not that they'd traveled into the future, but he knew they weren't at Bran's. They would have learned about his wedding much sooner if they'd only gone as far as the village. "Why did ye do so?"

"Because I could see that you were miserable, and I believed that Blaire was still in love with you, as well."

"And is she?" Arran turned away from her, his heart nearly stopping at the anticipation he felt at his question. It was wrong of him to ask, to care. He'd promised himself to another, but Blaire had claimed ownership of his heart long before he ever knew of Edana Kinnaird.

"Of course she is. She would never have dreamed of coming back here if she wasn't. We didn't know you were going to run off and get married. You don't love Edana, do you?"

"I'll not speak poorly of Edana, but I'll not lie to ye, either, and tell ye that I love her. It matters not. I am married to the lass, and there is nothing that can be done to change it." The truth of his own words hit him square in the chest, and he found himself leaning a hand against the wall to keep from doubling over. "Ye know the truth of my words. Why did ye bring her here if ye knew I couldna be with her?"

"Because things didn't end properly between the two of you. Now she needs closure, to know that it is finished and that you have both said your peace. You need it, too, Arran. Then you can both move on with your lives."

He inhaled deeply, trying to catch the breath that seemed lodged in between his ribs. "I shall go to Blaire. I must speak with her and see her once more before I lose her again. I've spent every moment since she left believing that I would never see her again. Now that she is back, I canna deny myself what I've been yearning for every moment. I know we canna be together, but I must see that she is well and apologize for the hurt I've caused her."

"Yes, go. But end it, Arran. Don't allow either of you to walk away, hoping for something that can no longer be. It would only make it harder for both of you."

He nodded, turning away from Bri as he silently opened the bedchamber door to make his leave.

***

*T*he ground behind me crunched, the coldness in the air hardening all of nature. The noise was a sure sign someone was approaching. Part of me hoped it would be Arran, but another part of me hoped that the footsteps behind me were a figment of my mind. I was furious, hurt, and humiliated by my presence here. It was wrong of me to have come to his home, to be in the place he shared with his new wife. But I wanted to see him, to hold him, to know that it wasn't only me that was pained by our last moments spent together before I traveled forward in time.

"Bri told me I would find ye here. I dinna think I would ever see ye again, Blaire."

My hand froze as it moved down the side of the chestnut-colored mare. "Aye, I suppose ye dinna."

"I'm pleased to see ye. It has been verra hard for me since ye went away."

He was lying, I was certain. Speaking words meant to make me weak in front of him and cause me to confess my true feelings. I'd done so once before, only to be sent away heartbroken. I wouldn't allow myself to be so foolish again. "Oh, has it? I dinna believe ye were that fond of me."

He grabbed me by the arm, pulling me away from the mare as he spun me so that I faced him. I was close to him, our chests nearly touching. Arran stared down at me angrily. "Doona do that, Blaire. I came here to apologize to ye, but I willna allow ye to behave as if ye believe that I dinna care for ye. Look into my eyes and tell me if ye believe that I doona still."

I held my breath. His grip on me was tight, and all I could see were his eyes, pained and hungry. My own chest started to rise and fall rapidly, and I yanked away from him. "Ye doona need to apologize for not wanting me. Ye canna help who ye love. I hope that ye and Edana will be verra happy together." I walked toward the stable doors as quickly as I could, desperate to get back to the safety of the castle. We were too alone here, and if he touched me again, I was afraid I wouldna be able to make myself push him away.

But Arran was too quick. This time he dinna only grab my arm but gripped me tightly by both wrists, pulling me back into the confined shelter of the stable. Once inside, he leaned against the door of an empty stall and pulled me against him, my wrists and front flush against his chest. I kept my hands clenched into fists, unwilling to allow my palms to rest against him, certain I would unravel at such an intimate touch.

He was tense, as if suppressing something deep within him. He didn't speak, didn't move. He only held me close to him as we stared silently at one another. Slowly, our breathing quickened, my chest matching the rise and fall of his. Arran's eyes dropped to my lips, only to dart upward again.

I felt danger rising, feelings unsaid threatening to express themselves through touch, and I squirmed within his grasp, hoping that I could move away and break the tension surrounding us.

He didn't allow it and only pulled me closer, leaning forward to plead breathlessly in my ear, "Doona move, lass." He pulled his head back so that his eyes pierced my own. "I know…I know I canna have ye, but ye were right. I canna help who I love and, married or not, I love ye, Blaire. I should never have sent ye away. To be separated from ye these past months has been hell. Ye have to know that I dinna mean a word I said before you went away. If I were a better man, I would never have done what I did to ye. If I were a better man, I wouldna allow myself to hold ye in my arms now."

His lips, trembling and warm, pressed against my forehead. I melted, allowing the man for whom I'd yearned for so long to hold me, as I'd dreamed of him doing for what seemed like ages.

I should've pulled away and run back to the safety of the castle. Around such company, he would never have been so bold, but here, with no one to serve as witness to our actions but our consciences, he held me tightly against him, his eyes hungry whenever they met mine, his body trembling as he struggled with his conflicting emotions.

My heart was beating such that I could scarcely think. Arran was a good man, an honorable man, a married man. I felt his struggle in the tension in his arms, hard muscles holding him back from surrender, back from the act that would undoubtedly sever his sacred marriage vows. Despite his past philandering ways, it was not in him to decide to do such a thing now that he had wed. It was not in me to ask him to betray his wife

He held back, his body as tight as a bow string. In that instant, I saw the future that lay ahead of me, one of solitude. Arran and I couldn't be together in the way we both desired, as husband and wife. But our love needed to be validated, to be expressed in such a way that we could both hold on to the memory that our hearts belonged to one another even as we made our way through life apart. I couldn't deny myself one kiss, one to take with me and cherish for the rest of my days and long, empty nights.

"Arran," I whispered his name softly, opening my fists so that the palms of my hands rested against his chest. It was enough—too much. He pulled away, his eyes red and heavy, glassy and moist with unshed tears. Although we stood apart now, he kept a tight grip on my wrists, silently pleading with me to send him away. But I could not.

"Aye, lass?" His voice was dry and cracked as the words struggled to find their way out of him.

"I know the truth of what yer marriage means for us, but I doona have the strength to walk away from ye this night without one kiss. Please, Arran."

He crushed his mouth to mine, his arms moving around me as he released my wrists and pulled me hard against him. I moved my hands up to the sides of his face, running my fingers through his hair as I heard him swallow a hard lump in the back of his throat.

I rubbed my thumb gently across his cheek, pausing as I touched a droplet of wetness that quickly found its way onto my tongue, its salty bite bringing tears to my own eyes. I'd known Arran all of my life, and had never seen him cry until now.

I pulled my lips away from his, and then kissed each one of

his eyes. He pulled away, rubbing his hands quickly over his face as he smiled, embarrassed that I knew he'd been crying. "I'm sorry, lass. What a fool I must look to ye."

I cupped either side of his face and kissed him gently. "Ye are not a fool. Ye are the man I love."

He smiled, the look in his eyes warming me all the way to my toes. "Aye, and you are the woman I love." His lips roamed over my face as he kissed my brows, my cheekbones, my chin. "I have been a frozen shell since ye left, Blaire. Tis only in this moment as I feel the warmth of yer skin that my heart begins to thaw."

I shut my eyes reveling in the feeling of his fingertips brushing against the skin on my face, my neck, my collarbone. I wanted so much more – we both did – but knew this would have to be enough.

"God, Blaire. Ye canna know how beautiful ye are."

Our lips met again with a heated passion, no longer restrained by our previous hesitation. With the knowledge that we could not be together in even this small way ever again, desperation filled us.

Our lips danced in a heartbreaking frenzy.

For a time, there was only this night, this moment, the two of us. All thoughts of tomorrow or yesterday faded, became as distant as the future that had separated us from each other for far too long.

CHAPTER 21

*A*rran, the fool, thought he and his lover had gone unseen, of that Tormod was certain. But he had kept a tight watch on the castle, waiting for anything he could use against the man who had stolen his birthright, and

his waiting had paid off. He'd long heard of Arran Conall's philandering ways, and such a man was unlikely to change his habits after marriage. Tormod couldn't have dreamed up a better partner for Arran's betrayal of Edana. For it wasn't just any woman with whom Arran was dallying; he had snuck into the stables with his brother's wife.

The two had handed him a grand opportunity, one if played properly would likely destroy both Conall brothers. Edana already hated them. Once he shared what he'd seen last night, Tormod knew she'd be willing to do whatever he asked of her to help him ruin them.

He waited inside the home he shared with his sister, watching for any sign of his pale-haired and plain-faced pawn to make her way through the village. She met him there each morning while Arran went on his daily ride. Their moments together were short, but each moment he was forced to spend in her company, talking and kissing, made him hate her all the more.

What a pathetic creature, so willingly giving him her trust at the first sign of his forced affection. She was ignorant, stupid, and Tormod found nothing less attractive in a woman.

"I see Edana coming this way," said his sister. "I shall be away now."

"Wait." Tormod called out for her to stop before she made her way out the door. "Do ye think 'tis wise to ask her to do what ye suggested? If she isna pregnant, Arran will surely know before too long."

Tormod flinched at the look Fia cast in his direction. "Aye, Arran will feel guilt over his betrayal of Edana, but 'tis not her place to forbid him his dalliances. If she tells him she's carrying his child, his remorse will multiply on its own, making him weak, just as we need him to be." She glanced away from Tormod, adding, "Edana is coming. Go kiss yer fool."

Once his sister left, Tormod moved to the doorway, looking each direction down the street to ensure that none would see the laird's wife enter his home. It was unlikely, he knew. People kept away from him and Fia. His sister's company was a pleasure most did not seek, for she was a woman of strength, not a woman of pity like the wretch that now made her way inside.

"Tormod."

He stiffened as Edana threw her arms around him. Pulling away from her, he motioned for her to sit next to him. "I have something to tell ye, Edana. Something we can finally use against Arran."

"Aye, are ye going to tell me that Arran has been with someone else? I know he dinna stay in his room."

Tormod's brows lifted in surprise. Perhaps the lass was visiting her husband's bed more often than he'd realized. It was all the better. It would make their tale all the more believable.

"Aye, he has, but not just with anyone. He spent the night with his brother's wife."

Edana shook her head, and Tormod lifted his brows even further. He'd been certain it was Eoin's wife he'd seen with Arran.

"Nay, 'twas not Bri, 'twas was the other one. Blaire. The one he couldna keep his eyes off of when they arrived. It seems that Donal MacChristy is more interesting than most people believed. He had two daughters, twins, and he sent one of them to grow up with his brother."

"Ye canna mean it? How could no one know of this?" His brows were about to lift off his head, and Tormod did his best to straighten his face into some semblance of normalcy. This was the most interested he'd ever been in Edana's words.

"They said that Donal was afraid he couldna care for both girls after their mother died. He sent Bri away, and she spent most of her life traveling in the care of her uncle, which goes a far way toward explaining the odd way in which she speaks. Blaire stayed here, and it was she that was supposed to marry Eoin. But before the wedding, Bri returned home, and it was she that Eoin fell in love with, not Blaire. But it seems that Arran has stepped in where his brother failed."

"I've never seen two lasses so similar in appearance." Tormod leaned back and shook his head in surprise.

"Aye, 'tis quite remarkable. But it was most certainly she that ye saw with Arran, not Bri. I saw Bri after I noticed that Arran was not in his room."

"Aye, I suppose it must have been. Regardless, I know what we must do to weaken Arran." He leaned forward and grabbed Edana's hands, knowing the effect his touch had on her. She yearned for him, and any intimacy he offered her, however slight, would only make her more amenable to his plan.

"What is it?" She stood from her chair and moved to his lap, looping her arms loosely around his neck. Tormod had to keep himself from grimacing as their bodies touched.

"Ye have been sharing his bed, aye?"

"Aye, but each time 'tis only ye that I see in my mind. Arran is only the vessel I use to reach ye when we are apart." She kissed him then, but Tormod cut the contact short, standing swiftly. "What is it?" Edana frowned. "Have I displeased ye?"

"No, no. You couldn't, lass." He touched her hair. "All's well and good. My mind is just preoccupied with my plan to overthrow yer husband. He should believe ye when ye tell him that ye are with child. I shall find a nurse to confirm yer story."

"Why? I am not with child, and it wouldna take too long before Arran would notice the lie." The pitch of her voice was high and painful to Tormod's ears. He turned away from her to grimace at the wall.

"By the time Arran would notice, ye may very well actually be with child, whether it be mine or his," he said. "And any remorse that Arran feels for having slept with another will only cause him more pain if he believes ye are carrying his child. His love for his unborn child and his guilt over betraying ye will make him weak." He could sense that she was about to protest. Rather than listen to the sound of her voice once again, he crushed himself to her and set about his daily task of making the fool love him.

onall Castle

"Slow down, Adelle," said Eoin. "I canna understand ye when ye speak so quickly."

Adelle threw her hands up in exasperation. Her son-in-law

was decidedly too calm over their present situation. It was clear that he hadn't heard her, or she was certain he would be much more panicked.

"Donal MacChristy is here. I've never seen a man who so closely resembles my ex-husband. I nearly jumped out of my skin when I saw him. He came to visit with Blaire. He said he wants to see her! I didn't know what to tell him so I just had Kip take him down to the stables so that they could get his horse situated." Adelle watched as her words sunk in, and Eoin's formerly calm face began to match her own.

"O'course he would show up whilst Bri is away. She canna even pretend to be Blaire if she isna here. How will I explain to him that his daughter went to visit my brother without me? He will hardly think it proper. And it isna! That's why she left without me. She knew I wouldna have let her go."

Adelle cleared her throat to interrupt him. "That isn't our only problem. When they do get back, how are we going to explain to him that there are two Blaires?"

CHAPTER 22

The Castle Formerly Known as Kinnaird

Morning came much too quickly, and with it the sadness that had been momentarily lifted slowly seeped back into my heart. As light started to peek through the small cracks in the stable doors, I felt Arran shift beside me, and I turned my head so that I could kiss his brow.

The tilt of my head sent a tear that sat dormant in the corner of my eye running down my face, and I quickly reached up to brush it away.

I'd not slept a wink through the night. Arran was too honorable a man to betray his marriage vows, and even if he hadn't been, I would not have let him. He would not have been able to live with himself had we made love. And so we simply held and kissed each other, which I knew was a betrayal of Edana, as well, if I were honest with myself. Sometime during the night, Arran had drifted away into the slumber of a man who'd not slept soundly in quite a long time. He'd held me tightly, squeezing his arms around me if I shifted only a little, as if he was afraid I would get up and leave him during the night.

Perhaps I should have, but my heart was torn into two very distinct pieces, and the confusion of feelings left me frozen and as trapped in the stables as I was trapped by Arran's heavy arms. I had never felt such love, such joy, never known just how deeply two souls could connect simply through touch. I had also never been so heartbroken. The sadness I felt at knowing what we shared could never be more – could not even continue as it was – caused me to ache all the way down to my bones.

"I doona wish to move from this place, lass. Do ye think we could hide away here and live with the horses?"

I smiled and kissed him lightly before forcing myself to stand and adjust my dress. "Nay, as much as I wish it, we canna. If I doona return before Mary awakes, ye know she shall have everyone in the castle looking for us."

"That she will, lass."

He stood, brushing hay and dust from his clothing, as I had done. "How will I get back into the castle unseen?" I asked him.

"I doona expect that anyone will question ye. If they do, just tell them ye went out for a morning walk. I shall leave from here to go out on my daily ride. I shall see ye, Mary and Bri before ye return home." He gathered me up in his arms, pulling me in so close that I could scarcely breathe. "I love ye, lass, and I doona believe that I can say goodbye to ye. When I am able to arrange it, I shall come to ye. From now on, my marriage to Edana will be only for her protection, but my heart shall always be yours. In time, Edana will learn to accept it. And perhaps she'll come to see that her happiness would be greater if she had her freedom. I would still watch over her, just—"

I stopped his words midsentence by tensing and pulling away from him, unsure of what he was suggesting. I couldn't have him make promises to me that I knew could never be. Arran was a good man, and though he spoke of a future freedom, he was not free now and never would be as long as they both lived – he and his wife. Soon, he would feel remorse for our actions. True, we had not consummated our love, but he had betrayed his wife, nonetheless, simply by holding me, kissing me, declaring his love. Once he admitted that to himself, he would not come to me again. "Tis best for ye to not leave me with hope when it isna there."

He grabbed me quickly, silencing me with his mouth, causing my head to spin and my knees to buckle. "I willna let ye go, Blaire. I canna do so again. Tell me that if I come for ye that ye will see me. I must live with the hope of holding ye in my arms once more."

The tears fell freely now. Any resistance I had shattered. If he came to me, I would welcome him. Though his honor and mine would not allow us to come together completely as lovers, I was not strong enough to deny myself the pleasure of his kisses, or the comfort I found in his arms. All that I was had been his for quite some time already. "Aye, I will. Now, leave. Bri and Mary will be awake soon. I should make my way back inside."

"I love ye, Blaire. When ye left this time, ye took my heart with ye, and it has belonged to no one else."

He kissed me once more, then moved to open the stable doors so he could mount his horse and depart on his ride. He smiled back at me as he left.

Once he was gone, I scanned the horizon. Seeing that all was clear, I made my way back to the castle.

*B*ri was awake when I arrived at our shared room. 'Twas apparent she'd been so for quite a while.

"Oh, Blaire. I'm glad you're back. I couldn't sleep a wink after Arran came by here looking for you. Are you okay?"

She stood from where she was seated on the edge of the bed and pulled me into a quick embrace.

"Aye, I shall be, in time. We should make our leave today."

She was kind enough not to question me further before going to wake Mary.

Once Bri had left, I cleaned myself using the small basin of water that sat at the back of the room. After changing, I did my best to pin my hair so that it didn't look like I spent the night in the stables.

I struggled with an unruly strand that was difficult to reach at the nape of my neck. It stuck out in a way that defied gravity, but unable to see it, I found myself useless when it came to securing it into place.

Bri entered the room. Seeing my difficulty, she came to offer her assistance. As she grabbed the long strand of hair, combing through it with her fingers, I asked her about Mary.

"Was she still sleeping when ye went to wake her?" While Bri worked on the back of my hair, I kept my hands busy trying to soothe the frizzing strands around my forehead.

"She was awake, but lounging in a steamy tub while three ladies waited on her hand and foot. Arran wasn't joking when he said she wasn't to lift a finger while she's here."

I laughed, picturing Mary ordering the poor lasses about. I was certain she would not be too pleased with having to leave Arran so soon. "What did she say to ye when ye told her we were leaving?"

Bri chuckled, and I caught her eyes in the small mirror before us. "Nothing that I wish to repeat. She said that we were welcome to leave if we wish, but she was making this her permanent home because Arran was the only one to show her any appreciation in ages. But don't worry, she'll come. In fact, I expect she will be ready for departure before us. Whether she will admit it or not, it's driving her crazy not to be ruling over her roost." Bri lowered her hands from my head and moved back. "There. Does that feel better?"

I reached behind and smiled as the piece was no longer floating toward the ceiling. "Aye," I said, nodding in approval. "Thank ye."

A knock at the door and Mary's boisterous voice from behind it signaled that Bri was right. Soon we would take our leave from the castle, from Arran, and from the place my heart would always remain.

---

*E*dana stood back after saying her own polite and expected farewells, watching closely as Arran made his own. He'd given her no explanation, made no excuse for his absence from his bedchamber the night before. Perhaps he thought she'd not come for him and believed his absence had gone unnoticed.

Even before Tormod's damning news, Edana had taken notice of her husband's empty bedchamber, and she'd suspected that he'd spent his night with another. She could not say she was surprised. The wandering ways of Arran Conall had been legendary as she was growing up, and she didn't know a single lass who didn't dream of having him woo her. But this knowledge did nothing to slow the torment of anger that spread its fiery touch over her each time she pictured them together. It didn't matter that she was in love with another. Arran was a fool.

It was only right that she should find a true man elsewhere, but she should have been enough for Arran.

At first, she'd been resistant to Tormod's suggestion that she lie to Arran about a pregnancy. But as she watched him lean into Blaire and pull her close, unable to stop his lips from lingering near her cheek and the undeniable yearning that shone in his eyes, she realized the awful truth. Arran had not only spent the night with Blaire, he'd given her his heart. Whatever loyalty Arran had once felt for Edana, it had diminished overnight. In order to keep him close, malleable to her plans, she had to regain his loyalty.

She would do as Tormod bid, and by sundown she would win back Arran's heart by pretending to be pregnant with his child.

CHAPTER 23

The first day of our journey back to Conall Castle was a pensive one. I remained wrapped in my own thoughts of loss and guilt. Although I had broken no vows to Edana, I couldn't deny the guilt I felt over her. She was an innocent victim of Arran's and my love for one another, albeit an unpleasant one. I'd only spent a few moments with her, but I was certain a friendship would never have been possible between us under any circumstance.

She was entirely miserable-looking, and something about her made me uneasy, as if she knew what had occurred between Arran and me. The glare Edana shot at me as we departed made me question whether or not my love and I had been alone the night before, as we'd believed.

The second day of our journey, the day we were due to arrive back at the castle, proved to be more eventful.

Mary complained regularly about us ending her rare treat of luxury so soon, but it was easy to detect the jest in her words. With each hoof step that brought us closer to Conall Castle, Mary's smile grew. I could tell she was itching to resume her duties as the true leader of the castle.

After at least a dozen complaints, she suddenly changed the subject and addressed me so bluntly that I nearly fell off my horse in surprise. "Ye slept with him, dinna ye?"

"Mary!" Bri's shocked and elevated voice echoed throughout the countryside.

"What?" Mary dismissed Bri's rebuke with a wave of her hand. "Ye have been thinking the same thing, have ye not? I saw the way Arran looked at her, and she at him, when we left. 'Twas not a look that people share unless they are intimately acquainted." Mary gave Bri an expression that dared her to disagree.

"I may have been thinking it, but I have the tact not to say it or ask," said Bri, cutting her eyes in my direction. "Goodness, Mary, I swear you get nosier with each passing day."

"I'm not nearly nosy enough!"

"Aye, we did sleep together, but not in the way that you think," I said. "I doona wish to discuss it further." I lifted my chin, knowing I'd merely piqued Mary's interest even more with my curious statement.

Mary narrowed her eyes at me. "What other way is there, lass? I wasn't born yesterday." She shook her head and smiled. "Doona ye worry, lass. I'll not be judging ye for it. Arran's marriage is not one built on love, and it never should have happened."

Sympathy was evident in her eyes, and it only increased my longing for Arran. It pained me to say it, but I couldn't bear for them to think that Arran had broken his holy promise to his wife. "I slept all night in his arms, Mary. But Arran did not dishonor his marriage vows any more than that," I said quietly.

Both women were unable to hide their surprise. Mary opened her mouth to say something but was interrupted by the appearance of

a rider off in the distance. We were nearing the castle, and Bri groaned and slowed the pace of her horse.

"Crap, it's Eoin. I bet he's so angry, he's ready to lock me away."

She laughed, but it was an uncomfortable sound. I could tell she was nervous for his reaction.

"Doona worry. He may be angry, but I've known the lad all his life," said Mary. "He knows by now that ye canna control women. He will just be glad that ye've returned. Besides, it looks as if he is riding for us. He must have news he hoped would reach us before we arrive back home."

Mary's revelation caused us all to pick up our pace in our eagerness to hear what Eoin had to say.

He met us quickly, reining to a halt beside us. "Ach! There ye are ye three naughty lassies. Why, I should throw the three of ye in the dungeon where ye canna cause any more trouble." He smiled, showing his jest. "But first, I want to kiss my wife. Come here, ye awful scoundrel." Eoin maneuvered his horse so that it was next to Bri's and deftly lifted her off her own horse so that she straddled him on his. He smacked her behind softly and proceeded to kiss her as Mary and I watched awkwardly.

Eventually Mary interrupted. "All right, that's enough! Stop it, the both of ye. I was feeling quite hungry and ready for a meal once we arrive back at the castle, but I think ye've spoiled my appetite."

"Hush, Mary. There's some remaining for ye, as well." Eoin dismounted, pulling Bri down from the horse with him. Once they were both on the ground, he moved to Mary's side, reaching for her and pulling her off the horse and into a tight embrace. He kissed her soundly on the cheek. She squealed and protested in his arms, but her red cheeks and wide smile showed her joy at reuniting with one of her boys.

"Tis good to see ye, as well, Blaire," Eoin said with a nod in my direction. "I'm glad ye have all arrived back safely, although ye should never have gone alone." Eoin set Mary on the ground and stepped away to regard us. "Ye left Adelle and me with quite a mess to trouble ourselves over. Not only our guests, but yer father arrived last night, as well."

"My father?" My voice croaked as I said the words. I hurried to dismount, afraid I might faint and fall to the ground, otherwise. As far as I knew, my father believed that it was I married to Eoin. He had no idea that I had spent the last months in a different century. He would have to be told the truth. Whether or not he would be able to believe it, I knew not.

"Aye, his arrival was unexpected. He said he was eager to see his daughter. I've done what I could to distract him, but he is verra disgruntled and losing patience. 'Tis best that we get all of ye back as quickly as possible so that the two of ye," he pointed to Bri and myself, "can give him whatever explanation ye choose."

"So ye told him nothing?" Part of me hoped Eoin would have explained everything to him, but it seemed that he'd left that unpleasant task undone. Not that I could blame him.

"Nay. I told him that ye'd accompanied Mary into the village to gather some supplies for the castle, and he was not too pleased to hear it. He thought it unwise of me to allow ye to go alone. I canna imagine what he would think of me if he learned I'd allowed ye to travel as far off as ye did."

Eoin ran his hand over his face, clearly exhausted after dealing with my father. I'd yet to see him, and fatigue was already overcoming me at the prospect.

He was a good man, and I loved him, but my independent spirit had made me a difficult child to manage. He'd been pleased when he'd finally been able to marry me off into the hands of another to oversee my behavior. He would not be pleased to know that his efforts had been unsuccessful. I was afraid he would feel it meant that he had ownership over me once more. If so, he would be disappointed. I would not be going back home with him, even if I had to work with Mary in the Conall's kitchens. I remounted my horse and gestured to Eoin, Bri, and Mary to do the same.

"Let's be on with it, then. I doona wish to keep him waiting."

"*I* canna believe it, truly. If ye dinna both stand before me now, I would never be able to believe such a story. I always knew Morna was a witch, but I never believed she would be capable of such a grand spell. Why, ye've given an old man the shock of his life."

My father laughed deeply as he gave me a warm hug. His reaction to our story after bringing him to the spell room was astonishing. Rather than doubt us or become angry, he'd accepted our explanation with pure curiosity.

"Ye are not angry with me?" I asked, returning his hug. "And ye will go along with what we told Edana, claiming us both as yer daughters?" It was a relief to be free of my nervousness over his being here. Now I could simply enjoy the feeling of safety that came with being wrapped in my father's arms.

"Nay, I'm not angry. I doona see how either of ye had a choice in what happened. And aye, I shall be pleased to call Bri as my own. I've thought she was for some time now." He smiled at Bri. "Ye did a remarkable job of fooling me. Ye are a magnificent trickster."

Bri laughed and shook her head in disagreement. "With all due respect, I believe your bad ear went a long way to making my performance believable to you."

"Ach, I'm sure ye are right, lass." Father reached up and touched his left ear.

Bri stood and excused herself to give us some privacy. We'd brought Father down here, hoping that the presence of Morna's spell books would help him to believe.

"I'll leave the two of you to visit alone for awhile," Bri said. "You know, I think it's fitting that I should be known as your daughter. You bear a striking resemblance to my real father."

She winked at both of us. Once she was gone, my father stood and grabbed my hand so that he could lead me out of the spell room.

"Let's go for a walk down by the sea, shall we? I'm anxious to hear of my bonny lass's adventures while she was away."

I nodded, and together we left hand-in-hand. In that moment, I felt closer to my father than I'd ever felt before.

CHAPTER 24

The Castle Formerly Known as Kinnaird

"Ye have been drinking less of late, have ye not?"

Edana's voice startled him. Arran turned away from the window he'd been staring out of, imagining where Blaire was, what she was doing, wondering if she was thinking of him, as well. One week had passed since she had returned to Conall Castle. Although she was days away, his world seemed brighter just knowing he could get to her, that she was no longer out of his reach in another century.

Every night since their departure, Edana had come to him, softly knocking on his door in the middle of the night. He'd ignored it, never giving explanation, hoping that within time she would give up and cease seeking his affection.

Tonight was the only night she'd entered his room uninvited. He faced her, doing his best to feign a smile. Over the past days, he'd come to learn more about his new wife, and what he'd discovered made it easier for him to push aside any guilt he felt over his feelings for Blaire.

Edana screamed at the servants and ordered them around as if they were criminals rather than loyal, hardworking members of their household. It was a habit she'd learned from her father, no doubt, but a needless act of malevolence, nonetheless.

Her moods shifted suddenly. It was impossible for him to tell when he was seeing glimpses of her true self. He hoped the real Edana was the one he saw in her rare moments of kindness, but something warned him that her other moments of ill-tempered outbursts ran deep to her core.

With each day, he grew more certain that she was not a shy, helpless victim, not a beaten woman who needed his aid, as he'd once believed. If only he'd not been so foolish, rushing into a commitment when he knew not to whom he was committing. He could be welcoming the woman he loved into his bed rather than denying his wife entry into it.

"Aye, ale is not so appealing to me as it once was. Why are ye awake so late in the evening, Edana?"

"I needed to speak to my husband. Have ye not heard me knocking on yer door these past nights? Have ye already guessed what it is I'm here to tell ye, and ye no longer find me so pleasing?"

He didn't know what she was talking about. He'd noticed little about her as of late. In fact, he hardly saw her when he looked right at her, so occupied his mind was with thoughts of Blaire. "Aye, lass, I heard ye knocking, but I have been tired. I have not been in the mood for company at night. But nay, I have not guessed anything about what ye have to say to me. What do ye mean by that?"

"I'm with child, Arran."

Shock coursed painfully through him, and he found that he was gripping the edge of the table so tightly that his knuckles shone white beneath his skin. "Nay, lass. We have not been married long enough for ye to be carrying a child. Even if ye were, it would be too soon for ye to know it." He hoped that he was right, but he knew little of such things, and he knew that his words were born more from wishful thinking than true knowledge.

"Aye, 'tis true that we have not been married long, but 'tis still verra possible for it to be so. I have not bled, and I have never missed doing so before. My nurse has confirmed it, as well."

Arran pulled the stool out from the small desk and plopped himself down on it, his head suddenly heavy and throbbing.

Edana motioned to someone standing in the doorway. Shortly after, a woman who looked to be about Mary's age approached him. She was short and slight. There were dark circles beneath her eyes. He thought she looked too unhealthy to be a nurse to anyone but still rose to greet her. Before he could speak, Edana interrupted.

"Go on, tell him. Tell him what ye just told me. That I am carrying his bairn."

Edana's tone caused him to look attentively toward the nurse who stood before him. There seemed to be an underlying threat with Edana's words, and the look of fear on the poor woman's face was enough for him to be sure he was right.

"May I speak to yer nurse alone for a moment, Edana?" He expected her response and fumbled quickly for an answer that would placate her.

"Do ye not believe me? What reason would I have to lie?"

"Nay, lass, I believe ye. If ye say that ye are with child, I believe that ye are. Tis only I have a private matter of a personal nature I would like to have seen." He smiled politely at the nurse.

Edana rolled her eyes as she slowly made her way toward the door. "Fine. Suit yerself, but ye know that she is not a real doctor.

She deals only with birthing and such matters. If something troubles ye, ye should see the man in the village."

"Tis only a small matter. I suppose any woman with knowledge of herbs could help me with this. Go on. I shall come to ye shortly, and we shall talk."

With Edana gone, Arran motioned for the nurse to sit on the stool in front of his desk. "What is yer name, miss?"

The woman's voice was quiet and shaky. It pained Arran to know that she must have been mistreated by the people of this castle for some time to be so frightened in his presence when he had given her no reason to distrust him.

"My name is Gara, and I'm afraid that she is right, sir. I doona know much of healing and only a little of herbs. Perhaps ye should seek help elsewhere. I wouldna want to mislead ye."

Arran crouched down in front of Gara, smiling to ease the woman's nerves. "Doona worry, lass. All is well with me. I only wanted to speak to ye without Edana being present. Now I wish that ye tell me the truth. Do ye know Edana to be with child?"

"Aye, sir."

"Ye doona have to worry, lass. If she's threatened ye, all ye need to do is tell me so. I'll believe ye, and I will ensure yer protection. Has she done so?"

Surprise flickered in the woman's eyes, and Arran allowed himself to hope that perhaps Edana's words had been a lie.

"Nay, sir. She is carrying yer child, as ye shall see soon enough. Now, may I be excused from ye, sir?"

Arran stood so that the woman could move from her seat and extended his arm out beside him. "Aye, lass. Ye are not being held against yer will. Thank ye for speaking to me and for yer honesty."

"'Tis my pleasure to be of service to ye, sir."

Gara stood and nodded before turning away from him, but

Arran called out to her once more before she could leave the room.

"I know that things have not always been good for the people of this castle, and while I claim no responsibility for yer suffering, I am sorry for it. I vow that I will do all I can to change things from now on. Doona ever be afraid in my presence."

"Thank ye, sir."

She slipped out quickly, leaving Arran alone to think about the unborn child that was seemingly on its way to him.

*G*ara hurried down the hallway, breathing in deeply and swiftly wiping at her face to hide the tears.

Arran Conall was a fine man. He would be a good laird to her and to her people. It did not sit well with her to lie to him, but she needed the payment for her family. The death of her husband had placed a burden on her that she'd been unable to adequately meet for some time. This lie would guarantee her family a roof over their heads for a long while. She was willing to put aside her morals for the sake of her children.

Still, it was not right, and she'd live with the guilt over such an injustice for all of her years to come. With each passing day, she would search for a way to make amends.

CHAPTER 25

"*D*id she do it, Tormod?" asked Fia.

He walked through the doorway of his home, not surprised to find his sister there waiting. She did her best to make him feel as if each new plan was his own, but he was no fool. He knew his puppet master well, and he needed her. Without Fia to guide him, he had no chance of destroying Arran Conall so that he could take over as laird and put a Kinnaird back in power over their territory.

She was talented at deceit and quick to think of each new step in their plan. He hoped today her ideas would be at their best. He had to find a way to rid himself of Edana for good.

"Aye, she told him last night, but his reaction was not what we had hoped. He was not so pleased to hear about his coming child."

Fia waved her hand dismissively in front of him. "Tis no matter to us. Such news is difficult for any man when the woman carrying his child is not the one he loves. The newness will wear away. Soon he will fall in love with the child, real or not. Why do ye look so upset, brother? The wretch did as ye bid, did she not?"

"Tis not enough to destroy Arran. I canna be with Edana. We

must rid ourselves of her and find another way to ruin Arran." Tormod paced around the room, frustrated and tired of his act with Edana. Each time he saw her, she clung closer to him. His patience was growing thin.

"Nay, ye are too filled with haste. As long as Arran believes that Edana is carrying his child, she is of use to us. If we were to end her life now, Arran would not have the attachment to the thought of a child as he will in a few months. When it comes time for her pregnancy to show, we shall release ye from her so that Arran doesna find out that she wasna truly carrying his child."

Tormod could see the sense in her words, but it did nothing to ease his impatience. Still, he would have to spend the months until Edana's death imagining it, savoring each image of her slowly taking her last breath. "How will we kill her when the time comes?"

His sister turned to him slowly, a smile spreading across her thin face that sent chills down his spine.

"I know a woman, a witch really. She has given me a poison that will kill Edana. When it comes time that Arran could see that she is not carrying his child, ye will give it to her and tell her that it is an herb that will make it appear as if she lost the child by starting a bleed. She willna know when she takes it that it shall kill her. When it is discovered that she is dead, it will look as if she died from an early labor with the child."

It would be perfect, far better than any plan Tormod could have devised on his own. Not only would the lass die in a way that would appear natural, but she would realize before she died that she'd been betrayed, that Tormod did not love her.

He could tolerate Edana a few months more. Then her perfectly tragic death would be the reward for his patience.

CHAPTER 26

*A*fter his conversation with Gara, Arran sat inside his bedchamber absorbed in his own thoughts of regret and self-pity. He knew it was wrong for him not to go to Edana, not to express to her how pleased he was that she was carrying his child, but he couldn't bring himself to lie to the lass anymore.

Their marriage was pretense, the reasons Arran had married her invalid. For Edana was not the woman she'd made herself out to be while staying at Conall Castle. Not only that, but each time he'd taken her to his bed, he'd been dreaming of another, a lass so special to him that the only children he'd ever imagined himself having were hers.

He was a man torn, sworn by law and his marriage oath that he would stay by Edana's side, but promised by soul and heart to a lass who was waiting for him at his brother's home.

He'd yet to seek out Blaire, afraid that each moment spent together would only make the moments apart more difficult. And now, with the news of his unborn child, he was afraid it would be impossible for him to go to Blaire without being crushed by the weight of his guilt.

If it were only Edana, his love for Blaire might have been

enough to push away his feelings of guilt. But now, with a child on the way, he knew he could not be unfaithful in any way.

Arran would not allow himself to be the sort of man to teach his children that such behavior was acceptable. It was bad enough the way he'd treated women before, using them for his enjoyment and then discarding them before his bed grew cold.

Blaire had changed him. He could now see the value of owning a woman's heart, the strength, responsibility, and the pure happy misery that came with possessing such a gift. He wanted to teach his sons to view women the same way, but he would be unable to do so if he continued to dishonor their mother through his relationship with Blaire.

It didn't matter that he did not love his wife. His conscience didn't care. It would be the hardest thing he would ever have to do, to give up his heart so quickly after having it returned to him. But his child would need a parent who lived a life of honor, more so than most if the child's mother was to be Edana Kinnaird.

He would tell Blaire face-to-face. It was the least he could do. His heart demanded that he see her one last time, to hold her and give her whatever explanation and apology he could offer. He knew nothing would be enough to heal the hurt he would cause her with his farewell. It had been she, after all, who'd tried to speak reason, saying that they should not meet again after their last night together.

He'd been a heedless fool. Unable to see the cards that fate would deal him when he'd promised Blaire he would come to her as often as he could. Now he would have to break her heart all over again.

His spirit broken, he sat down at his desk to pen a letter to her. He would tell her nothing of why he needed to see her, only ask that she meet him at the small cottage not far from Conall Castle in one week's time. She would come, her smile illuminating the four walls in which he would meet her. That smile he would soon snuff out, the smile he was afraid, once gone, would send him plummeting into the darkness he'd once known so well.

onall Castle

everal weeks had passed with no news from Arran. I found myself growing more certain that news would never come. I'd suspected as much when we'd said our goodbyes, but I hadn't realized how miserable waiting for him would be.

Despite Arran's promise that we would see each other again, I knew what kind of men the Conall lads were. I knew the kind of man their father had been. It would not set well with Arran to break his wedding vows, regardless of the quality of his marriage, and even if our relationship was only one of the heart and soul and never consummated.

For most, marriage had little to do with the love of the two people joined, anyway. Not in this time. One of the things I'd found most fascinating about the twenty-first century was one's ability to easily dissolve a marriage. If only Arran had married Edana there.

But he hadn't, and such a wish could never be. So as I continued to tear the handful of herbs Mary had given me, tossing them into the stew as she stirred, I talked to ease my mind of thoughts of loneliness.

"What do ye think of Adelle and my father? Do ye think that if they spent more time together, they could get on well?" I already knew the answer, but I also knew the reaction such a question would garner from Mary, so I let it slip out innocently, trying not to grin as I waited for her overzealous response.

Instead of Mary, Adelle's voice answered from the doorway. "Oh, gosh no, sweetheart. Your dad is a nice enough fellow, but truth be told, he looks so much like my ex-husband, it's hard for me to spend more than a few minutes in the same room with him."

I smiled and winked at Adelle as I nudged my head toward Mary. "Aye, I know. I only wanted to hear Mary ramble on about how ye do not deserve my father. If I dinna know better, I would say that Mary has taken a fancy to him herself."

Mary whacked her wooden spoon hard against the table. "And what of it if I find him to be a fine looking man? There's no harm in looking at him when he passes by. I dare either one of ye to spend forty-five years married to Kip and see if ye doona find other lads pleasing to the eye. Kip appreciates a pretty face, as well, and I'll not be one to deny him the pleasure of looking."

Adelle walked around the table and tugged on the sleeve of my dress, as if requesting that I accompany her. "Right you are, Mary. It's healthy to recognize beauty when you see it. I'd be lying if I said I wasn't green with envy over my daughter's new husband. Within the next few centuries, there'll be few men like him around."

I laughed and brushed my hands against each other to rid them of the remaining herbs. "I'll be back shortly, Mary, to help plate the meal for supper."

Mary nodded and turned her attention back to the stew. "Aye, that will be fine, lass. Ye know that ye doona have to be down here cooking away with me, anyway. I appreciate yer help, though."

Once we were outside the basement kitchen, I noticed the folded piece of parchment Adelle concealed in her hands. Flashing it before me, she waved it in the direction of the stairs.

Grabbing a lantern outside the kitchen door, we walked halfway down the flight of stairs before stopping to sit down on the steps next to one another.

"This came for you this morning. I saw the messenger riding in and went to greet him before nosier eyes saw it."

I couldn't repress an eye roll as I reached in the direction of the parchment. "As if ye are not the nosiest person in all of the keep, Adelle?"

"Well, I'll not disagree with you, but would you have rather Eoin retrieved it? It's from Arran."

My heart thumped painfully at the mention of his name, and I found that my hands were shaking as I snatched his letter from her hand. "I suppose ye will be waiting until I share what's inside of it with ye?"

Adelle nodded and grinned widely. "What kind of a question is that? Of course I will be waiting."

It took me little time to read the contents of his letter. It contained only a few lines of his jagged script. "He wants me to meet him at a cottage he says is near the castle grounds. I doona believe I've been there before." I paused, unsure how to express how I truly felt over his request. "I doona know if I should go."

Adelle sat quietly, as if thinking over the best advice to give me. "Do you want to see him, Blaire?"

The words slipped out easily, without hesitation. "Aye, o'course I do. I miss him every moment that I am not with him. But he is married, and I doona wish to tempt him to break his vows."

Adelle reached over and squeezed my hand gently. "You are making him do nothing. Would you like to hear my opinion? I'll only give it if you wish me to."

I nodded, enjoying the feeling of her hand around mine. I'd been small when my mother passed away, and Adelle was the closest thing I'd ever had to a mum. "Aye, I wish it greatly."

"I don't know how wise it would be for you to listen to an old, modern heathen like myself, so take what I have to say with a grain of salt. Relationships are far less black and white than some people wish to make them appear. There are some instances when life causes us to make decisions we wish we didn't have to make, but those things should not be used as an excuse to deny ourselves happiness. Arran's marriage to Edana was one of those decisions." She hesitated, as if unsure of how to express what was in her heart. "Do you understand what I'm saying?"

"Perhaps. Ye believe I should meet him, aye?"

She nodded slowly, squeezing my hand more tightly before standing. "If you want to, then yes. Don't deny yourself moments of joy with the one you love. It is Arran's decision to make, and it seems he has made it already by asking you to meet him. Guilt is a useless emotion. Do as your heart wishes. You will regret it when you're older if you do not."

She started back up the stairs, leaving me alone in the stairwell as I called up to her. "Thank ye, Adelle. I'm not sure if ye helped me at all, but I appreciate yer words nonetheless."

Adelle stopped at the top step and laughed loudly. "I'm not very good at advice. Ask Bri. She'll vouch to the truth in that. She was always more of a mother to me than I was to her. My point is that I regret the things that I didn't do more than the things that I did. And believe me, I was a wild child in my younger years. There weren't many things that I didn't do."

With that, she turned and left. I, though, continued to sit in the stairwell, allowing the candle inside the small lantern to burn away as I gripped tightly to Arran's written words.

Adelle was right. Even if it was the last night I could ever spend with him, I would regret not seeing Arran more than I would regret the guilt of our time spent in each other's arms. Besides, I'd promised him already that, if he sent for me, I would come.

CHAPTER 27

*C*onall Cottage

I arrived at the cottage just before sunset, knowing Arran would not arrive until after dark. The day after Arran's note had arrived, I'd ridden in search of the small cottage, finding it only a short distance away, in the direction of my father's castle. I couldn't believe I'd never seen it before during my many trips to Conall Castle as a small child, but Arran had chosen well. It was beautiful and secluded among the lush, steep hillsides.

I secured my horse and unloaded the basket of Mary's baked goods that I'd stolen from the kitchen just before leaving the castle. Making my way inside the one-roomed cottage, I started a fire and dusted out the rarely used room as best I could. I spread the food out on the small wooden table and was trying to catch a glimpse of my reflection from a sword that hung upon the wall when I heard the sound of a horse approaching outside.

However my face and hair appeared would have to do. Taking a deep breath for courage, I stepped outside to greet Arran.

He was as beautiful as I'd ever seen him. The last rays of sunlight cast down upon him as he rode in, illuminating his blonde hair and striking, deep blue eyes. He smiled, but it was not the unrestrained smile of excitement that I'd expected. Tension etched his face. And as he dismounted, I sensed that something was very wrong. His desire to meet me was not for the reason I'd believed.

Suddenly embarrassed by the spread I'd laid out for us inside, I moved to block his entry into the cottage, no longer wishing for him to see what I'd brought for us. He didn't say hello as he moved toward me, but silently pulled me into his arms as I stood in the doorway of the cottage.

He held me closely, not kissing me nor speaking as my head pressed snuggly against his chest. His hold frightened me. He clung to me as if he feared he would not ever see me again. "Arran." His name came out of me rather breathlessly. He held me that tightly. "Are ye well? Are ye ill or injured? Ye are frightening me."

I turned my head to look up at him as he finally loosened his hold and lowered his eyes to meet mine.

"Nay, lass, I am not ill or injured, and I dinna mean to frighten ye, but I am not so well, either."

"Come inside. 'Tis getting cold." I was no longer worried about him seeing the food spread out for him. He was far too troubled to notice.

I held onto his hand as I led him inside. We both sat on the edge of the bed that was against the back wall of the room. I turned to him, taking both of his hands into mine, each moment of silence a warning that my heart was about to break once more. "What is it, Arran? Ye canna stay silent any longer. What has happened?"

*H*e couldn't begin to know how to tell her what he must. The words lodged in his throat, content to stay there forever if his conscience would allow it. Once he said the words aloud, he would be forced to watch Blaire's heart break all over again, the same as it had the day she'd disappeared into another century.

He'd sworn that if he ever got her back, he would never let her go. That if it meant he would burn in hell, he would do so to be with her. But all of that was before his child came to be, an innocent in all of his mistakes. Arran could no longer allow himself to be selfish.

"May I kiss ye, lass? And then I will tell ye what I must, though I wish dearly that I dinna have to do so."

I nodded, but as his lips touched mine, the room grew colder. Instead of the warmth that his touch always evoked in me, an icy winter spread through my limbs, snapping every branch of hope I'd held for this evening spent with him. This was a kiss of goodbye, and my body rebelled against it. I pulled away from him, shaking my head as tears threatened. "Nay, Arran. I willna allow ye to do what ye are about to do. I canna lose ye again."

He stood abruptly, running his hands over his face and through his hair as he often did when he was nervous. He'd done so ever since he was a child. "I'm so verra sorry, lass. Ye canna know how much it pains me."

I stood as well, anger suddenly replacing any sadness. I'd known that he would be unable to live with the guilt, but why had he not agreed with me when I'd warned him our last time together? It was cruel of him to allow me to hope, only to destroy it once more. How many times could one man break and heal a heart?

I moved in front of him, shoving him as roughly as I could in the chest, determined to express my frustration and pain in any way other than tears. "Doona ye dare apologize to me. Why did ye ask me to come here only to tell me that ye can no longer do this? Ye had to know that I would believe ye were asking me to come and be with ye as ye promised me that ye would."

He grabbed me roughly by both arms.

"Perhaps I shouldna have asked ye to come here, but I couldna keep myself from seeing ye one last time."

I jerked out of his grasp. "Ye are selfish and cruel, Arran. What changed since I last saw ye? Ye should have told me then that we couldna be together, even if only to hold one another as we did that night. I knew ye were too good of a man to allow yerself to do even that any longer while married to another."

"Edana is with child."

'Twas not what I'd thought he would say, and the shock of his words must have shown on my face for he quickly continued.

"I expect my expression was quite similar to yers when she told me, lass. I have not touched Edana since I knew ye were back, but she says it happened shortly after our wedding."

I could think of little to say and slowly moved to sit down on the bed once more. "So that is why then? Ye can no longer meet with me for the sake of the child?"

"Aye, lass. I shall be a good man for my child, even if it shall break my own heart to do so, leaving me a shell of a man. If she wasna carrying my bairn, I swear to ye I would spend every moment possible with ye for the rest of my life."

He sat down next to me on the bed, crawling into the middle of it as he pulled me into his arms. Silently, I lay with my head against his chest, savoring the last moments I would hold him in my arms. I couldn't fault him for this. If he didn't act with honor now, he would not be the man who owned my heart.

"Can ye forgive me, lass?" He whispered the words into my hair as he gently kissed the top of my head.

"There is naught for me to forgive. Ye couldna have known I would return to ye, but I willna lie to ye and tell ye that my heart is not shattered, and I'm mighty jealous of yer wee wench of a wife."

He shifted in surprise, tilting my head up so that I was looking into his eyes. "Ye have nothing to be jealous of, love. 'Tis only ye that shall ever hold my heart."

I shook my head in disagreement. "Nay, ye are wrong. I'm not jealous of Edana, only that she carries yer child. If only we'd both not been so foolish, that was a joy meant for me. And I willna be the only one to hold yer heart. The child she carries will and already does, or ye would not be here ending this thing that is between us."

He couldn't argue. He knew the truth in what I said. Instead, he simply held me close to him, rubbing my back as his lips lay on top of my hair.

Eventually, I fell asleep. When I awoke the next morning to the first rays of light shining into the space around the doorway, Arran was gone.

CHAPTER 28

I was not surprised to find that he'd gone sometime in the night, but it made the finality of his farewell all the more painful. As far as I knew, there was no rush for me to get back to the castle, so I spent the morning inside the cottage with my arms wrapped around my knees, curled up in the bed, weeping.

I wept for Arran and his foolish choices that had gotten us to this point. I wept for myself and my ignorance. I wept so that once I gathered the strength to leave this place of refuge, so separated from anyone else, that I would not cry for Arran Conall ever again.

Midday, I rose and tidied things before splashing my face with the cold water from the washstand, scrubbing away any remnants of tears. The iciness of the water brought forth an idea. I quickly stepped outside to see if the weather would allow it. Summer was upon Scotland, and the weather, usually damp and cold, was now pleasant and tolerable. I twisted in my dress, missing the freedom that clothing in the twenty-first century had given me. Unfortunately, 'twas still many years before women would wear trousers.

I walked in a circle around the cottage to ensure my solitude as I set my mind to going out to the sea. A place I knew of along the beach on the way back to Conall Castle was just as secluded as the cottage. It had been years since I'd swum in the ocean; not that I had done it verra many times, anyway. The seawater was much too cold. But today it seemed a good idea, the appropriate medicine for my tender heart.

The water would hurt at first, its icy touch like a thousand pinpricks in my porcelain skin, but the pain would quickly fade and a numbness would replace it, a numbness that I hoped would work its way into my heart.

Ensuring that everything inside the cottage was just as it had been before my arrival, I mounted my horse and set out for the sea.

---

*A*s I'd expected, no one else enjoyed the shore. Although the waves were larger than I'd hoped, I was not going to let that keep me from a swim. I stripped bare, leaving my dress and underclothes on a mossy rock as I descended into the shallowest part of the water.

Two grassy hillsides on either side separated an inlet of ocean from the vast openness of the rest of the sea. A secluded strip of water, perfect for my chilling dip.

The first touch of water was so shocking I was afraid I'd pull my foot away to find that my toes had fallen off, frozen by the water's tight grip on a winter long over. The air outside might have begun to warm, but the ocean had yet to catch up to the changing of the seasons.

Intent on not changing my mind, I decided it was best to plunge right in, and I dove headfirst into the sea.

I'd expected the ocean depth to deepen quickly, but instead, my head cracked hard on a rock on the sea floor. As I pushed myself up to break the surface of the water, I reached up to touch my head and gasped as my hand came away covered in blood.

I could taste the saltiness of it dripping into my mouth. I struggled to catch my breath due to the frigid water. The sky began to swirl above me, and I feared I was bleeding heavily. Before I could drag myself out onto the shore, darkness closed in around me.

*T*he jostling of the horse that carried me caused me to open my eyes, but the effort that it took to do so sent such a pain travelling down my head and through my back that I shut them quickly once more.

I was naked; I could tell by the feeling of the horse's hair upon my calves. But I was discreetly covered by a tartan that I recognized as that of the Conalls' guests. "Where are my clothes?"

The man cradling me in his arms as he steered the horse answered softly, taking care that no loud noise would hurt my head further.

"I expect they are wherever ye left them, lass. I dinna take the time to look for them. Ye were bleeding something awful. I thought it best to get to ye before ye drowned or bled to death."

"Thank ye." The words sounded distant, as if it was not me that said them. Although I wondered who my rescuer might be, I was too weak for any more conversation. I could see Conall Castle up ahead, yet still I closed my eyes and drifted away once more.

he Castle Formerly Known as Kinnaird

ormod had not actually been in the castle since he was a small child, but he remembered the hallways well, and he had no trouble finding Edana's bedchamber.

Everyone in the castle was asleep and, if the rumors in the village were true, Arran Conall had been away for days visiting his brother at Conall Castle. For this reason, he'd decided to make this unexpected visit to Edana.

He knew Edana would be furious that Arran had gone and would assume that their plan to claim she was carrying Arran's child had not gone as hoped. It seemed she was right, but Tormod could not allow her to believe so. She had to continue to feign the pregnancy so that she could ignorantly take the poison at just the right time.

He knocked softly on her door, not wanting to draw attention from elsewhere within the castle. There were many men on duty, and he'd been lucky to make it so far undetected. It took a moment for Edana to answer. He couldn't keep his eyes from widening at the sight of her.

Her eyes were red, glassy. She was deep in her cups. Drunk. The longer he spent time with her, the more he knew that the lass had more in common with her father than she realized.

She stepped out of the way, nearly tripping, and Tormod quickly darted inside to help steady her. "What are ye doing, lass? Tis not appropriate for the lady of the castle to drink so much."

Edana sat down on the edge of her bed and patted the cover to suggest he should join her. "No one will know how I'm behaving. I am all alone here. My husband doesna care that I carry his child. He still finds time to visit his lover."

Tormod sat next to her, taking the goblet of ale from her hands. "Edana, ye are not really with his child."

"It doesna matter. The plan dinna work as ye hoped it would."

He forced himself to reach up and stroke her hair. "Just give it a while, lass. As time moves on, he will grow accustomed to the idea of a child, and he will love what he believes is growing inside of ye."

"And what will we do when he realizes that there is no child? Ye said we would think of something, but I canna continue to do this if I doona know that there is a safe way out of it. He canna know that we lied to him."

Tormod nodded and pulled his hand away. "Aye, lass, I know. 'Tis why I've come to ye. I have acquired an herbal drink that will make ye bleed when the time comes that Arran grows suspicious. It will appear as if ye lost the child. Then he will never know that ye dinna tell him the truth. He will only be lost in the grief of his unborn child. He will then be at his weakest."

"So it will do no harm to me?"

He stood and helped move her up higher onto the bed so that he could settle her for the night. Her eyelids were starting to droop. He was thankful that he would not have to take her into his arms this evening. "Nay, lass. It will do no more harm to ye than ye've done to yerself this night. Now, rest. I believe Arran is due to return home tomorrow."

Once her eyes closed, he slipped out silently, grinning at how easily she'd accepted his lie.

CHAPTER 29

"So you will stay then?" Bri and Adelle sat on either side of me, grinning, while a smiling Mary stood at the end of the bed. I gingerly nodded so as not to hurt my aching head.

It had been one week since I'd knocked myself unconscious during my ocean swim. While the wound on the top of my head was healing and hurting less, my chest worried me. It rattled with every breath I drew, and I felt more ill each day. I'd yet to mention my concerns to anyone; I had already caused them enough trouble.

"Aye. If ye will have me, I shall. I love my father, but I doona wish to return home with him. Have any of ye spoken to him about this? He will not be happy that I wish to stay here."

I watched as the three of them shared glances back and forth. Finally, Mary spoke up. "Aye, lass. He said that he would leave the decision to ye, but before ye make up yer mind, he has something else he wishes to speak to ye about. I believe he will be in shortly. 'Tis why we've come to ye now. We wished to ask ye to stay before he has a chance to talk to ye."

"And what is it that he wishes to ask me?" The rattling in my chest built. I swallowed hard to repress the cough that threatened to burst forth. I was being fussed over enough by these three ladies and didn't see reason to cause them more worry.

Standing, Adelle rolled her eyes dramatically, reddening with frustration. "He made us promise we wouldn't say anything to you, but I told him I think he's a fool for even bringing it up."

"Mom." Bri's voice served as a warning of the sound of footsteps approaching my room.

Baodan, Lady McMillan's eldest son and my watery savior, stepped inside the doorway, leaning his tall body into the wood frame. "Ach, excuse me. I dinna know that Blaire already had visitors. I shall take my leave and return at a later time."

"Oh, nonsense," said Bri. "We were all just leaving." She stood and smiled at me quickly before waving toward Adelle and Mary, indicating that they should follow her.

Adelle called back to me over her shoulder as they walked out of the room. "We'll be back this evening. I want to hear what you told your father."

I scooted back in the bed so that I could sit up straight. As Baodan approached me, he pulled his left hand out from behind his back, revealing my rumpled dress inside his grasp. "I will not disturb ye long, lass. I only wished to return this to ye. How are ye feeling?"

I took the dress, smiling at him in appreciation. "Thank ye. I feel much better. My head only aches a little now." As if to refute my claim, the cough that I'd held back earlier would no longer be repressed, and I lost myself in a fit of painful hacking that caused my head to pound severely.

Baodan quickly moved beside me, placing one hand on my

shoulder and another on my back to steady me. "There ye are, lass. Yer head may feel a wee bit better, but ye are not well, are ye? Have ye told anyone of this cough?"

I shook my head guiltily. "Nay, I havena. Tis nothing, I'm sure."

"Tis not nothing, lass. Ye breathed in too much of the cold sea water, and ill ye are. I'll send for someone to see to ye."

He moved away from me, and I instinctively reached out to grab his hand to stop him. "Nay, please doona do so. If it gets worse, I shall tell them, but I doona want a fuss over nothing."

"As ye wish, lass, but please promise me that ye will stay abed and rest until 'tis gone. I wished to speak with ye further, but I'll leave ye be for a while. Ye look as if ye could use some sleep."

"Fine, I promise. But what did ye wish to speak with me about?" I was curious, but he was right. I was exhausted, and the coughing had caused my head to ache dreadfully.

"Tis not urgent that I speak to ye about it now. We'll have time to do so later." He smiled at the confused expression on my face and ducked his head as he retreated from the room.

Twas the first time I'd actually spoken to Baodan alone aside from the moment on the horse, but I wasna nearly conscious enough then for that to constitute conversation. I couldn't imagine what he seemed so keen to discuss with me.

I quickly drifted into a restless and short-lived sleep, stirring as I felt my father's lips lightly touch my forehead.

"Ye scared me badly, Blaire. When Baodan rode up with ye, yer head bleeding so fiercely, I thought for a moment I would lose ye. Ye are all I had after yer mother died. I canna bear the thought of losing ye, as well."

I reached up to dash away a rogue tear running down his face, and he quickly grunted in embarrassment. "Ach, I am not a crying man, but a father's love for his children is enough to bring a man to his knees. How are ye feeling, love?"

"Better." I dinna say more, not trusting my cough to stay silent otherwise.

"I'm sure that Bri, Mary, and Adelle have already been to see ye. Did they tell ye what I've come to speak with ye about?"

"Nay, but Adelle seemed none too pleased about it."

Father smirked rather uncharacteristically. "Aye, I suppose she dinna. She's a strange lass, but I canna say that I doona like her. She's fiery like ye, Blaire. I am glad that she was there to take care of ye in yer time away."

I smiled. "Aye, me too. Now what is it, Father?" A small cough escaped, but I was able to hold off any more so that it seemed as if I had only cleared my throat.

Intuitively, he stood and moved to the water basin to pour me some water. Returning to my side, he said, "Baodan has asked me for permission to marry ye."

I spit up all of the water in my mouth. "What?" I struggled to get the word out in between a fit of coughing.

Worry creased Father's brow as he scooted in closer, cradling me as Baodan had done earlier. Eventually, the coughing subsided and father shook his head in dismay. "That must be seen to, lass."

I dinna argue as I had done earlier. He was right. Each fit of coughing grew louder and lasted longer than the time before. "What did ye just tell me, Da?"

"Baodan came to me a few days ago and asked permission to marry ye."

"Why would he do such a thing? Are ye sure that ye dinna arrange this? Ye did it once before. What did ye tell him?"

He took both of my hands in his own, stroking them tenderly. "Nay, lass, I did no such thing. I was wrong before to send ye here to wed Eoin, but please believe me, I only did it because I thought it best for ye."

"I know." And I did know. I was the most precious thing in the world to him. He was simply at a loss as to what to do with me.

"I told him the choice was yers, lass. I will not make such a decision for ye again."

That was at least some relief. "Thank ye. Ye doona think that I should do it, do ye, Father?"

He looked down and shrugged. "I doona know, lass, but I believe him to be a good man." Meeting my gaze again, he asked, "What will ye do if ye doona marry? Ye are welcome to return home, but I doona believe that ye wish to do so. What is here for ye? Ye were not meant to work in the Conall's house. Ye deserve a family and keep of yer own."

His question was fair, but one I'd given little thought to. "I'm unsure, Father. But I doona know Baodan. I doubt I could ever love him."

"Ye canna know that for sure, lass. I dinna love yer mother at all when we married, but she was my very soul by the time she left this world. I will not advise ye what to do. Ye are a sharp lass. I shall let ye decide. All I ask is that ye think on it. Speak with him. Get to know him before the McMillans leave in three days time."

I nodded, unsure of what to say. Father could tell that I needed rest. He bent to kiss me once more. "I love ye, lass. Sleep now and think of it come morning."

After tucking the blankets around me, he poured more water into my cup then blew out the candles, leaving me in darkness. Before sleep finally took me, I lay awake for hours, all that he'd said turning over in my mind.

CHAPTER 30

The Roadside Inn – Present Day

"What's the matter, love? What have ye seen?"

Morna jumped at the sound of her husband's voice. Slowly she opened her eyes, pulling herself out of the dream. "Ach, Jerry. It doesna seem to matter how often I help them, they always find a pathway to trouble."

He sat with her, wrapping his frail, bony arms around her as she'd known he would, acting as the supporter he'd always been for her. "Who, lass? What has happened?"

"Blaire is verra sick. I doona think she will heal on her own. She needs modern medicine to keep her from dying. I believe Bri will look for a way to heal her. If I can only leave something in the spell room for her, she will find it without having to travel forward. It takes a toll on the body, and I doona think Bri should go through again."

"Why dinna ye say so, love? Give me what ye need to leave for her, and I shall go at once. I know ye doona like to return to the castle. I'll go and be back in time for supper."

Morna stood and kissed her husband firmly on the mouth. "I knew there was a reason I married ye."

Leaving him smiling in the living room, she went in search of the antibiotics and all of the other medications needed to rid Blaire of the sickness that threatened her life.

---

1 646

By the next morning, I was coughing up blood and my skin was so warm to the touch that sweat covered my body. I drifted in and out of sleep, delirious, nonsensical dreams dancing before my eyes.

When the visions stayed present while awake, my worry increased. My vision remained constantly blurred, and I could hardly register when someone was in the room with me or when water was being poured down my throat. I knew that someone stayed in my company, washing me, trying to coax me to eat, changing my sweaty bedclothes and bloodied cough rags, but didn't know who. I could hardly speak, I was so overcome with fever. And I couldn't move without the aid of another.

Fluid built deep within my lungs. I knew death was coming for me.

Each morning, Bri would come to dose me with medicine. Advil that she'd brought back with her the last time she'd passed through the portal. It helped in breaking the fever only for a little while. With each passing day, the medicine seemed to burn off more quickly, and I found myself in delirium once more.

On the fourth morning, I prepared myself to say my goodbyes. The fever had receded slightly, and only one person demanded the forefront of my mind. After Bri came to administer the pills, I asked her to stay so that I could take advantage of what I assumed would be a brief respite from my delirium.

Knowing I would not last long, I gave quick instructions. "Bri, I need ye to get me some parchment and a pen. I need to write to Arran and tell him what is happening. I need him to come and say goodbye."

I could sense that Bri wanted to argue, but she looked me over and held her tongue. She, too, could tell that there was not much life left in me. I scribbled the note with haste, grimacing when a slight splatter of blood landed on the parchment as I coughed. I handed it over to her, and she sealed it without reading, respecting my privacy, as I'd known she would.

"Ye will send someone with it right away, aye?"

She nodded and placed a moist rag on my forehead. "Of course I will. Now rest. I'll take it to a messenger now."

"Thank ye." I shut my eyes as she left, feeling more peaceful than I had in days. I only had to hold on until Arran could came and bid me farewell.

***

$\mathcal{B}$ri ran through the castle and out the back doors in search of Kip, calling out to him before she even reached the stables. "Kip, can you call one of the lads that helps you with the horses straight away? I need one of them to ride to Arran."

She slowed her pace as she rounded the corner into the stable to find Kip already ordering a young lad to mount up for the ride.

"He shall take good care of it. Won't ye, lad?"

The boy nodded, and Bri gratefully handed the parchment up to him, only pausing to kiss Kip lightly on the cheek before taking off at a full run back to the castle. It was time for her to enter the spell room again. She'd be damned before she let Blaire die.

Flying through the castle, Bri nearly slipped on the steps leading down into the basement. She recovered quickly, not pausing to catch her breath until she stared, open-mouthed, into the contents of Morna's spell room.

Sitting on top of the spell book was everything they needed— syringes filled with antibiotics, more Advil, medicine to break up the fluid in Blaire's chest. All of it sat atop the faded, yellow parchment as if it had always been there.

She almost turned to stop the messenger, but decided it best to let him go. Modern medicines would help greatly, but as sick as Blaire was, she didn't know if it would be enough to save her. In case they didn't, she couldn't deny Blaire's last wish to see Arran.

Smiling, Bri moved into the spell room to gather up the treasures. Morna's days of magic had not ended with their last trip into the past. She was watching over the Conalls and her beloved home still, centuries away from them all.

The messenger rode fast, only stopping for a few hours of rest and to relieve himself when necessary. He'd seen the panic in the lady's eyes as she'd brought the parchment to him. He knew not what information Arran Conall needed so desperately, but the lad's family had been loyal to the Conalls for decades. He would not be the first of his people to disappoint them.

He made the journey in half the time it would have taken most. Knowing his horse was in desperate need of rest, he stopped at the edge of the village and knocked on a stranger's door to see if he could pay for a stall for his horse while he attended to his duty.

***

$\mathcal{T}$he knock on the door surprised Tormod. Surely Edana would not be visiting at this time of day, and everyone else in the village knew better than to come to his home. He swung the door open to find a travel-weary young lad with dirt on his face and clothing.

"What do ye want?" Tormod stared down at the lad, hoping that his size alone would be enough to strike fear in the boy.

"Excuse me, sir. I'm travelling from Conall Keep and am on my way to deliver a message to yer laird. I was only hoping ye would allow my horse to rest here for a bit whilst I complete my task."

"Conall Keep, ye say? Let me see this note that ye carry." The boy backed away from him, and Tormod floundered for an explanation for his request. "I only want to make sure that ye come from where ye say, and then I shall return the letter to ye and allow yer horse to rest here."

Hesitation crossed the boy's face, but eventually he extended the parchment toward Tormod. Tormod snatched it out of the lad's hand before ripping it open to read its contents. He then tossed the letter into the fire.

The boy lunged at him, but Tormod caught him swiftly by the throat, pushing him into the wall. "I suggest ye get on yer horse and ride back to Conall Castle. Tell whoever sent ye that ye delivered their message just as intended. Ye would not want them thinking that ye failed them, would ye?"

The boy shook uncontrollably under Tormod's heavy hands, and his face looked conflicted as he took in his words. "Aye, sir. Ye are right. If ye will only allow me to leave, I shall do as ye ask."

"O'course ye will, lad. Now get out of here and doona ever knock on my door again. Understand?"

The lad nodded and quickly mounted his horse, fleeing in the direction of Conall Castle. Tormod smiled ghoulishly as he shut the door. Not only was Arran about to lose his wife and child but his lover, as well. And he would believe she died without him bidding her farewell.

Everything was beginning to lean in his favor.

wo months had passed since the day Bri, Adelle, and Mary had come charging into my room and rather excitedly poked me in the bum with some sort of sharp instrument. That day and the days following, I'd been too overcome with fever to question or worry about what it was they were doing to me. Eventually, though, the fever broke for the last time. Slowly but surely, I started regaining my health.

Still, there was no doubt just how close to death I'd come. People seemed nervous around me, avoiding much in the way of conversation, as if they were afraid I would break if touched or spoken to. I'd still not left my bedchamber. The closest to the outdoors I'd come were the few short moments each morning that someone helped me to the window, where I sat and enjoyed the summer breeze.

Only the past few weeks were fresh in my memory, but I knew my days had settled into the same routine for months. Mary brought meals throughout the day, staying with me to ensure that I finished every bite. Afterward, she told me stories while combing my hair or rubbing my feet.

Each morning, my father visited, but he only stayed a short

while before heading out to help Eoin with whatever task needed doing. He would not return home until I was well, but he refused to be a guest in the Conall home without contributing in some way to their well-being.

The afternoons were spent with Bri and Adelle. This was my favorite time of day, for the two women were the only ones who had enough faith in Morna's medicines not to tiptoe around me, fearing that any stress might cause my death. They talked freely, and I usually ended up laughing so much that the coughing fits returned. Whenever that happened, Mary appeared to shoo them from the room.

I could tell by the angle of light through the window that it was almost time for Bri and Adelle to arrive. As if summoned by magic, they appeared just as they crossed my mind.

"Hello, hello!" Adelle clapped her hands together, smiling broadly. "You look much better today, hon. Soon it will be time for you to get outside and stretch your legs. It's certainly nice enough for you to do so, and you've spent so much time in bed. It's important for you to start rebuilding your muscle strength. I'm sure you're as weak as a new babe. I think tomorrow one of us will get you outside." She moved across the room to open the window wide, allowing the sunlight and fresh air to seep inside.

"I'll not argue with ye. My legs have shriveled away to nothing. Come and sit with me."

Both ladies hiked up their dresses and sat with their legs crisscrossed on the end of the bed.

"Mom's right. You're looking much better." Bri laughed as she patted me lightly on the knee. "What did you think that first night I came and stuck that needle in your rear end?"

"I dinna know what ye were doing, but I was far too ill to care. Truthfully, I doona remember much of these past months. Only the past few weeks are clear to me."

Adelle fidgeted, and I could tell she had something she really wanted to say but didn't know if she should.

"What is it, Adelle? Please doona be like Mary and speak to me like I might die from real conversation."

Adelle laughed and stopped bouncing the bed with her jittery movements. "Fine. What have you decided about Baodan? You do remember your father telling you that Baodan asked him for your hand in marriage, right?"

"Aye, I do remember, but Father has not mentioned it again, and Baodan does not speak of it when he visits. He has come to sit with me each evening the past few nights, but says little." I nibbled my lower lip and frowned. "I'm not so keen to bring up his proposal."

Bri's brows drew together as she studied me. "Is that all you remember of your time with Baodan? Only the last few days?"

"Aye, is there more that I should remember? If there is, I am lost to it. The fever made everything a dream."

Bri stood and went to shut the door to my bedchamber so that no passerby would hear our conversation. "Yes, but I'm not surprised that you don't remember it. Baodan has been at your side every day. When you were at your worst, it was he that replaced your bloodied rags with clean ones and lifted you so that we could clean you and change your bedding. He wiped your cheeks with a wet cloth and brushed the hair out of your face, only leaving you when we instructed him that he must. It's only been since you've been more yourself that he's stopped visiting as often."

It was surprising to me that he'd done so, and I didn't understand his reasons. "Does he feel that much guilt over what happened, do ye think? Twas not his fault. I jumped into the water all on my own. If he'd not been there, I would've died that day."

Adelle shook her head. "No, I don't think he feels guilty. I think he's quite taken with you, dear. I think perhaps I was wrong to react the way I did to your father's news that Baodan wants to marry you." Adelle winced with remorse.

I felt the heat of a blush creep up my neck. "What are ye saying, Adelle? Ye believe I should marry him? He's not even asked me. Perhaps he's changed his mind."

"I'm not saying you should agree to marriage. Not yet. Just get to know him. See if anything is there between the two of you. And I don't think he's changed his mind. I heard him asking Mary earlier if he could take you for a short ride tomorrow, just the two of you. Go with him and think about whatever he says to you. I think he's a good man. It's rare to see someone be so attentive when he hardly knows you."

"Mom's right," Bri agreed. "He's been incredibly caring toward you. But Blaire, just know that you are welcome to stay here forever if you wish. Truly. Do not say yes to him because you feel you have no other choice." She stood and motioned to her mother to do the same. "We should go. I expect he will be along shortly."

I called out to stop Bri from departing, hoping to speak to her alone about the one thing that had hung at the edge of my mind even during the worst of my fever. "Wait, Bri. Can I speak to ye a moment alone?"

"Of course." Bri stepped back inside, and Adelle waved at me before disappearing through the doorway. Sitting on the chair next to my bed, Bri crossed her legs. "What's up?"

I hesitated, not wanting to show how much I cared what her answer would be. "Arran... did he...did he come at all while I was ill?"

I knew she would not lie to me. As I'd hoped, she answered without hesitation. "No, he didn't. And he sent no letter back in response to yours."

"Is it possible that he dinna receive it? Mayhap the messenger lost it along the way."

Bri blinked sad eyes at me. "No, I'm so sorry, but I spoke to the messenger we sent myself after he returned. He told me that he delivered it to Arran's hands directly. The man has no reason to lie."

"Aye, I suppose 'tis true. Thank ye. That's all I needed to know. If ye doona mind, I'd like to be alone now."

Bri stood and nodded once. "Absolutely. I'll see you in the morning. Get some rest."

She'd only just made it to the doorway when Baodan appeared, and they passed each other as she made her way out of my room. He smiled at me but remained in the doorway. I was thankful; it seemed he would not be staying long.

"I'm sorry I dinna come to see ye earlier today," Baodan said. "I've been working on something for ye that kept me away. Do ye think ye would feel up to accompanying me somewhere tomorrow? We willna go far from the castle, and I've received Mary's blessing to get ye out of doors for awhile."

Images of Arran reading my note, learning that I was dying, and choosing not to come to my side, pierced my heart. He was truly gone from my life. I pushed away the pain and smiled as brightly as I could at Baodan. "Aye, I would like that verra much."

"I am pleased to hear it, lass. I will see you soon, then."

With a nod, he ducked under the doorway and left. I rolled over so I could stare into the setting sun. Perhaps the light would burn all images of Arran from my mind.

CHAPTER 32

Mary lay the dress she'd picked out for me over the back of the chair next to my bed then pulled back the curtain so that the morning light streamed in. "Nay, lass. I doona think 'tis a good idea for ye to strain yerself by bathing right before ye go outside. The outing will be hard enough on its own."

"Do ye want me to call for Adelle and Bri, or will ye oblige and help me yerself? I'm sure they would be more than happy to do it."

"Nay, lass," Mary said, sounding flustered. "Please doona go hollering, ye will only make Adelle do the same. If ye insist, I shall have a bath drawn for ye, and if ye wish to wear another dress I shall retrieve it."

I smiled triumphantly as I pushed myself upright and swung my shaky legs over the side of the bed. "I insist. I doona wish to be proposed to while looking a mess. And I can smell myself. It has been far too long since I've had more than a cloth bath."

"Aye, fine. I do agree that ye smell a wee bit like old cheese. Do ye have any other demands of me?"

Mary feigned annoyance, but I could tell she was happy to

help and glad that I was feeling well enough to bathe. "Aye, can ye have Bri and Adelle come? I'd like Bri to pin up my hair, and Adelle willna like it if she is left out of the preparations."

"Aye, I suppose ye are right about that, as well. Give me a moment. I shall fetch them."

"No need," came Adelle's voice from the doorway. "We're here. We saw Baodan this morning, and he told us you agreed to accompany him. We thought we would come and help you get ready."

Adelle crossed the room and gave me a light hug. Then she helped me to my feet as a smiling Bri extended a treasure in my direction.

"Look what I've brought for you! I went down into the spell room and retrieved it from your pile of modern clothes. It will make you feel more human, and you'll like what it does to the way your dress looks."

"Aye, I know. It can work miracles." I reached for the bra, pressing it tightly to my chest. "But do ye not think that he will notice it?"

Adelle laughed heartily, garnering a lower-yer-voice-before-I-thump-ye look from Mary. "If it was me accompanying Baodan today, then yes, he might. But I don't think you're the sort of girl to let a man pass a base on the first date."

"Base?" Mary and I said in unison, sending both Bri and Adelle into a fit of laughter.

"Never mind, dear," exclaimed Adelle between snorts. "Let's start getting you cleaned up."

Adelle led me toward the tub while Mary instructed the men who brought in steaming pails of water. Before long, I was being tugged and pushed and prodded in different directions as all three women worked diligently to prepare me for the outing.

The Castle Formerly Known as Kinnaird

If Arran was counting correctly, Edana should have been swelling more beneath her clothing than she seemed to be. It was true that he was no expert in such matters, but it had been at least four and a half moons since he'd shared her bed, and he could not see the slightest change in her physical appearance.

He'd also taken notice of how well she seemed to be feeling. She'd not been troubled by the bouts of ill stomach he knew many women suffered during their beginning stages of being with child. It had been bothering him for days, the wondering, and he knew he could not keep his questions at bay any longer.

He reached across the table where they sat while eating their evening meal. Placing his hand gently on her shoulder, he said, "Edana, I wish to ask ye something, but I doona want ye to be angry at the question."

She sat back in her chair, malice clear in her eyes. Each day he could sense her disdain for him a little more sharply.

"Why would ye think I should get angry? Are ye suggesting that I'm angry often?"

There was no reason to be gentle with her. Arran knew that regardless of what he said, Edana would find a reason to be upset by his words. "Aye. Exactly. Ye stay angry all the time. Ye scream at people who have done naught but help ye, and I believe ye are a liar."

Her face blanched, and something deep within told him his suspicions were right.

"What do ye mean?" she said, her voice so low and breathless he almost didn't hear the question. "What could I have lied to ye about?"

"I doona believe ye are with child, Edana. Ye havena swollen at all, and it has been too long for ye not to have done so."

She pushed away from the table and stood, and Arran could see that her hands shook with rage. "I canna believe that ye would insult me so," she said, her voice rising. "'Tis only that ye canna see how I've grown with my clothes on. Kinnaird women never swell much with their children."

Arran stood, as well, his confidence in his suspicion growing with every word she uttered. "Aye? Is that so, lass? Fine. Why doona ye take yer dress off right here and show me how yer belly grows?"

She stepped away from him, as if afraid he would rip her dress right off of her body. He couldn't deny he was tempted, but he was not the sort of man to disgrace a woman in such a way. Besides, he didn't need to. Her reaction was more than enough to make him certain she was not carrying his child.

"I'll do no such thing, ye wretched man. Do ye think ye cannot touch me for months and then have me take my clothes off? I willna allow ye to do so. When yer child arrives, ye will see what an ignorant fool ye have been."

She turned her back on him and fled the room.

Eoin did not go after her. He sat down to finish his meal. She was right about one thing. He was a fool. A fool to have ever believed his wretched wife, and a fool to have denied the one woman who had ever truly loved him. Deep down in his soul, he had sensed from the beginning that Edana had lied to him, from the very night she'd come to him with news of their child.

Whatever misery life with Edana would bring to him, tonight he felt as if he deserved every bit of it.

A knock sounded at Tormod's door. If it was the Conall messenger again, he decided he would kill him. Surely the lad wouldn't be so foolish as to knock upon his door twice. And not so late. Night had long since settled over the village.

Tormod opened the door and was nearly knocked to the floor as Edana threw her arms around him, weeping. "Arran knows. He knows I am not carrying his child."

He unwrapped her arms from his neck and pushed her away from him. "Slow down, lass. What do ye mean? Did ye tell him?"

His face flushed with anger at the thought. If she'd been so stupid, he would kill her this night. If she'd ruined their plan with her words, he would not put up with her one moment more.

"Nay, I dinna tell him anything, but he told me that he doesna believe that I am carrying his child. He has noticed that my belly hasna grown, and he thinks I have lied to him."

He turned away from her to grab the glass bottle he'd patiently held onto for months. "Then doona worry, lass. All is fine. If he suspects that ye are lying, it only means that now is the time for ye to take the herbs. Once he believes ye have lost the child, he will blame himself for upsetting ye so. Here." He gave her the bottle. "Take it tonight, lass, once ye are abed. Take every last drop. I shall see ye in a few days after all is done."

Again, she wrapped her arms around him, kissing him quickly on the cheek. "Aye, I shall drink it as soon as I return to the castle. I love ye, Tormod."

He opened the door to show her outside. "Aye, lass, I know ye do."

Once she'd departed, he shut the door and waited. When he was sure she'd be far enough ahead of him that he could follow her unnoticed, he left the house. This promised to be a wonderful night. Edana's death was finally upon him.

CHAPTER 33

*E*dana took her time returning to the castle after obtaining the herbal solution from Tormod. She wandered the streets of her small village, the only home she'd ever known, battling an inexplicable sense of unease. The village and the people in it came alive for her in a way they never had before, as if she were saying goodbye.

As a young girl, she'd taken after her mother. She'd had a sweet spirit and never understood why her father became angry when she played with the children in the village. She couldn't see the difference between herself and the people that lived under her father's protection outside of the castle walls.

She'd had many friends. Her mother ensured it, taking her out daily to interact with the people of the village, doing her best to make sure Edana understood how blessed she was to live a life in which things came to her easily.

If only her mother had lived, Edana suspected that she would have become a better woman—a woman like her mother. Her father had always been a terrible man, but her mother's death released him from his cage. When that happened, darkness descended over her life.

Her father had never allowed her to leave the castle. Surrounded by the evil that seeped from him, Edana had sensed that her soul was beginning to warp. Her thinking changed, too. The people who had been her childhood friends began to seem unworthy of her attention. She was a Kinnaird, and there were few worthy of her time.

Tonight she felt a shift in that mindset she'd held for so long. As she passed the candlelit windows, she wished she could join the people behind them. To live a simple life, free from the ghosts of her father, was a dream Edana had long since stopped allowing herself to hope for.

But perhaps Tormod was right, and once Arran was gone, she would be free. Together she and Tormod could create the simple life she longed for. He had to be right. Her trust in him was the only thing that kept her moving closer to the castle, even as a small voice in the back of her mind told her to smash the bottle onto the ground and flee from her life here.

Arran spoke the truth when he said that she was easily angered, but it pained her to have it stated so plainly. She wished she could change, but she knew she could not. Her father's grip held tight inside her still, and words of anger and hate slipped off her tongue when words of kindness would not.

She was tired of not being the person she wanted to be. As she entered the castle and climbed the steps to her bedchamber, she vowed to herself that once Arran was gone, she would put all of the past behind her and start anew.

Her bedchamber was empty, as she knew it would be, but she felt uncomfortable at the unease she felt at finding it so. If Arran had decided to wait for her there, she would have been unable to take the herbal solution.

She set the bottle down next to her bed, undressed, and then donned her nightgown. Crawling into bed, she propped the feather pillows so she could sit up. When Arran found her there, it would appear that she'd been in pain and forced to endure an early labor on her own.

Edana knew she would have to drink the contents of the bottle quickly so that she would have time to stash it away, out of sight, before the bleeding began. Once she'd bled enough to raise alarm, she would scream for someone to come to her aid. She only hoped the cramping wouldn't be too painful.

Shaking, she reached for the glass bottle, then wiggled the top off. The scent was potent, and it made her stomach churn. It smelled nothing like any herbs she'd been around, but she was uneducated in such matters. There was no reason for her to believe that the mixture was anything other than what Tormod had told her.

Pinching her nose, she touched the bottle to her lips and quickly tilted it upward. She had to swallow hard and fast to keep from immediately retching out onto the bed. Once she'd drained the bottle's contents, she bent over to place the vial under the bed. She resumed her position—legs spread wide apart—and waited for the bleeding to begin.

At first nothing happened. Other than the foul taste in her mouth, she thought perhaps the process would be a painless one. But just as quickly as she'd begun to hope, a pain settled deep in her belly. She opened her mouth to scream, only to find that no sound would emerge.

The pain spread fast. Fire seared through every inch of her body. Holes burned through every vital organ. Finally, the sounds came—inhuman moans—so quiet she wondered if her vocal chords had melted when the potion touched them.

She glanced down between her thighs to see blood draining out of her, and knew. Poison. Not the herbal mixture Tormod had promised her.

Just as quickly as the pain had begun, it stopped. Her heart beat slowly in her ears. Her limbs hung lifeless and cold. Blood continued to drain from her body as she realized the mistakes she had made. So many mistakes.

Her father's spirit had never coaxed her to seek revenge on the Conalls. Instead, his spirit had rooted for her demise. The same black presence he'd been in her life had cheerfully led her to her death.

What a fool she'd been to believe Tormod. To believe that a man could love her and want to care for her. To want him to—a man no better than her father.

The one soul who could've given her all she needed, and who would've kindly done so even though he didn't love her, was the man she was about to hurt the most.

Arran would not know that she'd done this to herself. That she'd lied. Once he found her, Edana knew Arran would blame himself and live with the guilt always, a fate he did not deserve. She'd been too foolish to admit that before.

She took her last breath, praying that Arran would one day learn the truth.

Her prayer didn't include herself. She got no less than she'd earned. Casting aside her hopes for a new life, Edana shut her eyes as death took her.

onall Castle

We'd all expected that Baodan would call for me sometime in the morning, but as the day passed with no sign of him, we quickly learned that we were not as sure of his plans as we thought.

I was ready before midday, all cleaned up, hair pinned back, looking as presentable as I had in months with nowhere yet to go. The morning's preparations exhausted me, so shortly after I was ready, and Bri, Adelle, and Mary were satisfied with my appearance, I lay down and fell quickly asleep.

It felt as if I'd only drifted for a few short moments, but when I awoke to the feeling of a hand lightly grabbing my own, I opened my eyes to see the light from the setting sun fading out my window.

"I'm sorry, lass. I should have been more specific as to when I planned to come for ye. I feel terrible that ye've spent the whole day waiting on me. Ye must be exhausted already."

I was, but I sat up with as much energy as I could manage. I swung my feet over the bed and stood, only slightly shaky. "Nay, doona be sorry. I needed to get up and behave as a human for a while."

I was certain the back of my hair was a mess after sleeping on it most of the day, but I didn't want to fix it in front of him. What did it matter, anyway? I had no real feelings for Baodan; there was no reason to try and impress him.

"Are ye ready, lass? If ye doona feel like ye are ready to leave the castle for a bit, we doona have to go. I wouldna like for ye to make yerself sick again by doing more than ye are ready to do."

I reached up to grab his arm, the thought of spending one more moment in my bedchamber torturous. "Aye, I couldna be more ready to get outdoors for a while. I shall gladly go wherever ye wish to take me."

"That is my hope, lass."

His words made me nervous, and I instantly regretted my previous enthusiasm. I didn't want to make him believe I felt something I did not. If he intended to ask me what everyone around me seemed to think he was going to, I had no answer for him.

I didn't know the man well enough to love him and, even if I grew to know him well, I was certain my heart was not capable of surrendering to another. Regardless of Bri's insistence that I was welcome to stay at the castle as long as I wished, I knew it would not be right to live a lifetime with her family, relying on their charity and friendship.

And Father was right. Even if I could not have the love that I longed for, I did still someday want children—a notion which, before Arran, I had found repulsive. I used to think the idea of children a dreadful thing, but Arran's love had opened a part of me I had not known existed, and even though he was gone from my life, those parts of my soul remained open.

Baodan held tightly onto my hand as we moved slowly down the castle stairs, stopping often to allow me to rest, each step a struggle after being off of my feet for so long.

There was no question that Baodan was a good man. I knew Arran well enough to know that he would not have been as patient with me, and I did not get the feeling that Baodan struggled with drink as Arran sometimes did. Baodan would be a good father. Perhaps if I did not want to be alone forever, Baodan would be a fine choice of a man with whom to spend my life.

I set my mind to consider the possibility. I would listen to all he had to say and hope that the right decision would come to me.

---

*B*aodan lifted me onto his horse with ease. Whether I wanted to or not, I was forced to lean back against him. My muscles were so weak and tired. I trembled terribly from the effort it took just to make it out of the castle.

My weak muscles were enough to make me shake, but within moments of leaving, I became certain I knew where we were headed. Not that Baodan could have known I'd been there before. It wasn't possible that he knew the memories this place would bring up for me, the pain that I had suffered here. No one at the castle, save Adelle, would have known that I'd been here before, and I was certain she didn't know that the cottage was where Baodan planned to take me.

He'd been here today, readying it for this evening. Candles burned inside the windows. The entire place was alight with the soft glow of tiny flames.

Baodan reined in the horse next to the cottage, dismounted, and then carefully helped me down. He continued to hold on to both of my elbows, helping to steady me as he led me inside.

"If I know the three lassies that spend every spare moment by yer side, I expect ye already have some idea as to why I've brought ye here. But I doona wish to speak of that right away. First, I'd like simply to share a meal with ye and visit so that we may get to know one another a bit more. Would that be acceptable to ye, lass?"

"Aye, it would." I sat down in the chair he pulled away from the table for me. I did my best to push away all memories I had of the last time I'd been here.

As soon we started eating, Baodan said, "I know that I do not know ye well, lass, and ye do not know me, either. But 'tis my ardent wish that we both grow to know each other better."

"Aye? Well, anything ye wish to know, I shall tell ye. Many think I am much too free with what I say." The food was delicious, and I relished in the enjoyment of eating at a table rather than in bed.

"I do not mind straightforwardness in a lass. My beloved wife was much the same way."

I certainly had not suspected that he'd been married before. While I knew him to be at least five years older than me, he did not look it. To imagine him with a wife in the past proved difficult.

"I did not know that ye were once married. How did she go, Baodan?" My wording was off, but I was unsure of how to ask what I wanted to know in a way that wasn't rude or painful. I was sure he would understand my meaning well enough, though, and I was right.

"How did I lose her, lass?" Briefly, he closed his eyes. "Six years ago, 'tis been. We'd only been married a year when the sickness came for her. I was away on a short trip, gone for only a fortnight to help a man with acquiring a piece of land. I knew not that she'd been ill until I returned home to find her dead. I live with the guilt of not being there with her those last days."

That went a long ways toward explaining his attentiveness while I was so ill, and I felt uncomfortable at the thought that my stupidity had caused him to relive such pain. "I'm verra sorry. I doona know what else to say to ye, save that."

He shook his head and took a deep breath, pushing the dark memories away, it seemed. "There is naught to say but that, but I appreciate yer kindness. I thought that ye should know before I ask ye what I intend. Yer father has spoken to ye of it, aye?"

I nodded, swallowing my mouthful of food and scooting my plate away so that I would not be tempted to eat more. "He has, but if ye intend to ask it, I'd prefer to hear it from ye, as well."

He smiled and stood, dragging his chair so it was in front of mine. Then, resuming his seat, Baodan gathered both of my hands in his. "Aye, lass, that would only be right of me, would it not? I shall ask ye what I asked yer father, but I wish to be honest with ye first, if ye would allow me to be so."

"O'course. I would wish nothing less than whatever truth ye have to give."

"I am not in love with ye, lass, and I doona know if I ever will be. My heart was buried with my wife long ago, but that doesna mean that I doona want a family, and I doona wish to spend the rest of my days alone."

He paused, but held my gaze, as if unsure he should continue. "Go on," I coaxed. "Say whatever ye wish, and I will take no offense to it." Truthfully, I was pleased that he dinna offer a confession of love. It would have been unkind of me to accept it when I had none that I could return to him.

"Verra well, lass. I've heard some talk that ye yerself have lost a love. Nay on purpose, but yer three bonny friends doona speak as quietly as they sometimes think they do. I've come to believe that perhaps yer heart is in much the same place as mine, that it belongs to another and always shall. There was one name that ye whispered during yer fevers over and over again, and I doona wish to cause ye pain by speaking it here."

My intake of breath was sharp, and he could see that he'd surprised me. "I did not know that I'd done so. Bri, Adelle, and Mary never said."

"I know that ye did not, lass, and I doubt that they were privy to seeing ye do so, as well. They were often with ye only when ye were awake. I was afraid to speak much with ye, so I kept ye company often while ye slept."

"Ah."

He laughed softly before continuing. "Perhaps, I should have kept that to myself, aye? That may be unsettling to ye, but I assure ye, lass, I was only watching over ye to make sure ye were safe and as comfortable as ye could be."

I squeezed his hand. "Aye, I know. It comforts me that I was so well watched after. Thank ye. I have not told ye thank ye enough for saving my life."

"I deserve no thanks, lass. Any man but the worst would have done the same. But this is really what I've brought ye here to ask of ye." He fidgeted nervously, and I rubbed my thumb back and forth across his hand to calm him. He smiled as he looked down at our entwined fingers. "I believe we are both of similar hearts and minds, lass. While I know I canna give ye what ye once had, I can give ye companionship. And I swear to ye that I will offer ye protection and a happy home. As for any children that we may have together, I will love them and serve them for all of my days. Will ye marry me, Blaire?"

Arran was gone. Whether he was happy in his marriage or not, he was now expecting his own child. When he'd said goodbye to me the last time I was in this cottage, he'd certainly meant it. Even word that I might die was not enough to bring him back to my side.

Baodan was a more honorable man than the one who owned my heart, and I would not be lucky enough to come by a better offer ever again. "Aye, lad. I'll marry ye."

He smiled as he leaned hesitantly forward, gently sealing my promise with a kiss.

CHAPTER 35

The Castle Formerly Known As Kinnaird

Arran woke in the middle of the night, his heart beating quickly, panicked and filled with a sense of dread. He rose, drenched in sweat, and paced around the room to try and calm his breathing.

He couldn't understand what caused him to feel this way. He was a sound sleeper, and he'd not been having nightmares. Just the opposite, actually. Blaire had come to him in his dreams, as she did most nights. He delighted in the time he spent there holding her in his arms, kissing her over and over again. No matter how unreal or fleeting those moments were each night, he clung to them, wishing each day away so that nighttime would come and he could be with the woman he loved once more.

But tonight his dreams were interrupted. He could not shake the feeling that something was terribly wrong. He dressed quickly, then opened the door to his bedchamber so he could listen for any sign of trouble that might be brewing below the stairs.

The castle was silent and dark, save for a few candles still burning. Reaching for the candle closest to him, he hesitantly made his way out into the hall. He knew not why he was headed her direction, but every step forward brought him closer to Edana's bedchamber.

The lass should have been asleep long before now, and he knew he should not disturb her without reason, but something deep inside him lurched with fear as he stood before her room. He pressed his ear against the outside of the door, hoping to hear her snoring or moving about.

When he heard nothing, he breathed deeply and quietly pushed open the door. He looked first not at the bed, but at the candles, still lit, scattered throughout the room. It was unlike her to leave them burning after she'd gone to bed. Perhaps she still had not returned to the castle. He knew he'd angered her greatly in the dining hall.

Slightly relieved, he stepped all the way inside and had to swallow hard to choke down the bile that rose in the back of his throat.

Her head lay oddly back against the pillow, the upper half of her body propped up, as if she were sitting. Her eyes were wide open and lifeless, her legs spread awkwardly open. It was then Arran noticed the blood slowly dripping off the end of the bed.

A deep, animalistic groan escaped his throat at the gruesome sight, and he fell to his knees in the doorway. He knew not how long he sat there, but eventually the castle began to stir. He was pulled to his feet by two servants, but he quickly jerked away from them and fled the room, not stopping until he burst outside the castle doors.

With his first deep breath of the cool air, he vomited, then sobs overtook him. He knew it was his fault. The lass hadn't lied to him about the baby, and his screams and horrible accusations had caused her to lose the child, and ultimately her own life.

How soon after he'd gone to bed had Edana fallen ill and begun to bleed all alone in her bedchamber? How long had she suffered before dying? The questions that tormented him made him ill. No one, not even Edana, deserved to die such a death, all alone with no one to come and provide aid to her or answer her cries for help.

She must've screamed. How could one not when going through pain such as that which was so clearly etched forever on her face? If only he'd drunk less during their last meal together, perhaps he wouldn't have been sleeping so deeply not to hear her cries.

Arran knew he was not a good man. Not like his brother, not like his father. He'd battled demons of guilt and remorse for past decisions for much of his adult life, but nothing compared to this transgression for which he would now have to hold himself accountable.

He'd killed her. Whether it was by his own hand or not, he knew he would feel responsible for the lass's death and for the death of his unborn child for the rest of his life. Rising, he straightened himself, roughly brushing away his tears. The least he could do for her now was to see her properly laid to rest. Then he would beg God for forgiveness for all that he'd done.

Making his way back inside the castle, he began giving orders, stopping the castle's messenger as he passed him on the stairwell. "Ride for Conall Castle at once, lad. Speak only to my brother, Eoin, and let him know of what has passed here this night. He will wish to be here as we lay Edana to rest."

*T*ormod watched from his hiding place just on the edge of the castle gates. He'd left shortly after Edana, silently following behind her so that he could keep tight watch on the castle. He wanted to know the instant his plan succeeded.

It had taken longer than he'd expected. Eventually, he'd drifted off the sleep as he crouched low to the ground, out of sight from anyone who might pass by him. Late into the night, a cold breeze stirred him. Tormod looked up to see the castle slowly fill with light. He suspected then that someone had found Edana's dead body.

He hoped that was the case. He still wasn't sure if the lass had found the nerve to go through with the plan. She'd been quite shaken earlier when she knew that Arran suspected her lie.

It wasn't until he saw Arran's shadow burst through the castle doors, saw him retch all over the ground, that Tormod knew for certain Edana was dead.

He was finally free of the young, foolish, ignorant lass, and his soul smiled at the knowledge of it.

Tormod remained in his hiding spot, watching the activity in the castle throughout the night, enjoying every moment of knowing how Arran would blame himself for his wife's death for the rest of his life. The plan had played out exactly as his sister had predicted. Arran would be at his most weak and vulnerable in the weeks ahead.

There would be many in the village that would find Edana's sudden death surprising. All Tormod had to do now was plant the seed of suspicion as to the cause of it. If he could make the townspeople turn on their new leader , it would go a long way toward ensuring his own place as laird once he did away with Arran Conall once and for all.

He was so close to all that he wanted he could almost taste it.

Ridding himself of the wretched Edana had been the hardest part. His sister would know just the right way to proceed to finish his task. Within a fortnight, he planned to be residing within the very castle he was lurking outside of now.

CHAPTER 36

onall Castle

"So you said aye to him, love?" asked Father. "And ye are at peace with yer decision?"

He appeared at my doorway late in the night, shortly after we returned from the cottage. I'd just made my way to bed. It was clear that he'd waited up so he could learn of my decision.

"Aye, Da, I did. 'Tis the answer ye hoped I would give him, is it not?"

He surprised me by shaking his head. "Nay, lass. I did not wish for ye to say aye if 'twas not what ye wanted, but I cannot deny that I am pleased that ye will be taken care of. Baodan is a good man. He will treat ye well."

So tired I could scarcely keep my eyes open, I yawned widely, speaking to him in between deep breaths. "Aye, I believe he will."

"Well, I'm happy for ye, lass. Baodan is anxious for ye to marry so he can take ye away to yer new home up in the

McMillan territory. If it pleases ye, I told him I'd like ye to be married at home."

"Aye, I would like that verra much."

"Good, lass. We shall all set out the day after tomorrow – the McMillans, the Conalls, and us. Sleep well, daughter."

He turned and left, and I chuckled lightly to myself. He was more pleased than he cared to let on that I was to be married. He'd been quick to make the arrangements, not wanting me to run out on another wedding.

The Castle Formerly Known as Kinnaird

Gara waited until all of the other servants were to bed in the wee hours of the morning, after Edana's bedchamber had been cleaned and her body removed for burial preparation, to seek out Arran. She knew the new laird would not sleep tonight.

For the sake of her family, she'd done as Tormod and Edana had bid her. But she had not known the malice behind their plan. She'd gone to assist in the cleaning of Edana's room once she heard news of the lady's death, and as she'd bent to scrub the pool of blood off the floor, Gara had spotted the small bottle turned over on its side.

She'd picked it up, tucking it away as she tried to understand why the poor lass would've done something so vile to herself. Then she noticed from where on Edana's body the blood had come, and realized that her death had not been self-inflicted.

It was Tormod who'd killed her. The monster had played Edana for a fool, and she'd fallen for it, drinking the solution as he bid her. She must have thought it would feign the loss of the child so that Arran would not find out she'd lied to him.

Gara's realization caused her to fear Tormod even more, and she slipped the bottle away so no one else would see it. But her guilt over the lie she'd told for him was more than she could bear. She couldn't allow Arran to be fooled by his wife's deceit – and her own – and forever blame himself. Perhaps she could tell him the truth about the child without revealing the real cause of Edana's death.

———

*A*t first Arran thought he imagined the knock at his door. The previous commotion throughout the castle had long since settled, and he'd assumed he was the only one still awake. When the soft rapping began again, he moved from his stupor of self-loathing and guilt to see who was at the door.

When he opened it to find Gara, he was certain she'd come to tell him what he already knew – that Edana's death was no one's fault but his own.

"Verra sorry to disturb ye, sir, so late and especially on this night. May I speak to ye a moment?"

He stepped away to grant her entry. "Aye, o'course ye can. What is it, lass?"

Her gaze lowered. "Before, sir. I lied to ye."

He was too tired to think of what the lass could have lied to him about. "What do ye mean, Gara?"

"The night Edana brought me to ye months ago, she was not carrying yer child. Not that night, not this one, either."

"What?" Her words hit him square in the chest. They were too much for his sleepy, guilty, grief-stricken mind to absorb.

"I'm telling ye that Edana lied to ye, sir. She was not expecting a child."

"If that's true, lass, then how did she die?"

"I doona know, sir. Women sometimes do bleed unexpectedly. She just lost too much blood too quickly."

Arran paced around the room, unsure of how to take what the lass was telling him. He was hesitant to believe her, even though he himself had questioned Edana for so long. "How can ye be certain that she was not with child?"

"I examined her myself. There was no child inside her. Never was."

Relief washed over him. He was not pleased by Edana's death, but if what Gara told him was true, at least he could rest in the knowledge that it was not he that had caused it, and there had not been a child lost, as well.

"Thank ye, lass. So when ye told me she had not threatened ye, I suppose ye also lied about that, aye?"

"Aye. I could not risk her harming my children, sir, and we were in desperate need of the payment she gave me. I apologize for any hurt I have caused ye."

"Doona worry. It was not yer fault. I'll not speak ill of the dead, but it was wrong of Edana to have ye do so." He placed a hand on her wrist. "Before ye go…"

She stared at him hesitantly. "Aye?"

"Is there more ye are not telling me, lass?" Arran needed desperately to know everything. "Anything else ye can share about why this happened?"

Her eyes grew wider as she shook her head in denial. "Nothing at all," she whispered.

He nodded. "Then ye may leave me now."

After Gara departed, Arran sat alone in his bedchamber, wrestling with a flurry of emotions. To go so quickly from overwhelming guilt and loss to possible relief and optimism about his future brought on a different sense of guilt.

He had known that Edana was a horrible person. But now,

after Gara's admission, he realized he had not imagined just how low his wife had been willing to stoop in order to have her way. Still, it felt wrong for him to feel relief because she was dead.

The lass had lied to him for some time. He couldn't deny that he'd lost respect for her long ago. Still, he would lay his wife to rest. Anyone deserved that much.

He was now free from a union that should never have been. As soon as he saw Edana laid peacefully to rest, he would ride to Conall Castle to retrieve his heart.

To retrieve Blaire.

CHAPTER 37

onall Castle

rran spent the few days leading up to Edana's burial in solitude, silently making peace with her death and his own regrettable decisions that had linked him to her. But now that he knew the truth of Edana's lies, he realized there was only so much responsibility he could take in what happened to her.

He would not allow himself to be haunted by her any longer. Once she was buried, he rode immediately for his home. He'd been surprised when Eoin had not come to be with him after receiving the news of Edana's death. He'd carried out the burial quickly, so perhaps his brother simply hadn't had time. Arran would explain it all to Eoin upon arriving home.

Some of his new clansmen would undoubtedly question how he could move on so quickly to a new wife, but Arran believed that anyone who'd spent time in Edana's company, or that of her father's, would understand.

He couldn't wait to see Blaire, to run to her and beg her to come back to him now that they could truly be together as husband and wife. They could have the family they'd long dreamed of having together.

Arran nudged his horse with the back of his heels when he saw the stables ahead of him. He was so close. Only a few more moments and he would be able to hold her again.

He rode into the stables at full speed, pulling up hard on the reins so he could fling himself off the side of his horse. He didn't notice Kip standing in the corner until he heard the old stable master's voice.

"Arran, 'tis good to see ye, lad, but what brings ye here? The castle is empty save myself and a few other servants."

Arran walked toward Kip and clasped his dear friend on both shoulders. "Have they gone down to shoot arrows then?"

Confusion filled him as he watched Kip shake his head. Where else could everyone have gone? Not far, surely. "Where can I find them?"

"Slow down, lad. I'll ask ye again. Why have ye come here? I only just received word about yer wife three days past. I'm truly sorry, lad."

Kip's words brought back the sharp pain of Edana's death. No matter how he'd felt about her, he could not help but regret the loss of someone so young. If only she'd had the time, he thought perhaps she could've become a better person than she was when she died. "Ach, thank ye, Kip. But ye know as well as I that I should not have married her in the first place. 'Twas an awful mistake, and one that I doona wish to repeat by allowing myself to spend one more moment apart from the lass I'm meant to marry. Where is she, Kip? Where's Blaire?"

Arran's nerves built as he watched Kip turn his face downward and awkwardly pick at the ground with his foot. Kip hesitated to tell him something, and it frightened Arran greatly.

"What is it, Kip? Doona tell me that something has happened to her. Is she well? Ye must tell me at once."

"Nay, lad, naught has happened to the lass, but she is not here. She's at MacChristy Castle with the rest of yer family. She's set to marry yer cousin Baodan in two days."

"What? How could this happen?" Arran set to mount his horse, not wanting to stay a moment where Blaire was not.

"What do ye mean, lad? He asked her, I suppose."

"So, she doesna know of what's happened to Edana?" He turned the horse in the stables so that he could ride in the direction of MacChristy Castle.

"I do not know, lad. She may by now, but I was the only one here when the messenger arrived with the news. I sent him straight for MacChristy Castle to find Eoin. He is probably just arriving."

Arran spurred the horse forward, calling back to Kip over his shoulder. "Thank ye, Kip. I shall see ye soon. I doona intend on staying away from Conall Castle so long ever again."

*M*acChristy Castle

*T*he messenger arrived late in the evening on the day before I was to marry Baodan. I was away in my old bedchamber with Bri. She was playing with my hair, teasing it into different arrangements for the wedding, when Adelle burst through the door, red-faced and breathless.

"Mom, what is it?"

Bri dropped the strands of my hair and rushed to her

mother's side. Certain something was terribly wrong, I nervously twisted in my seat so that I could face her.

"Edana is dead. The man Kip sent with the message said that her child tried to come early. Both she and the baby have died."

The room suddenly felt much too small. As tears threatened, I stood to make my way outside, but Bri reached out and grabbed my hand to stop me. I didn't know what to think of Edana's death. I'd been so jealous of her for having Arran when I could not, for carrying his child. But I would not have wished such a fate upon anyone.

"Blaire, are you all right?" Bri asked quietly.

I nodded and pulled out of her grasp. "Aye, only sad. Arran does not deserve such pain. Does Eoin know?"

Adelle nodded. Addressing Bri, she said, "Yes, he plans to ride out in the morning. He shall miss the wedding, but he wishes to be at his brother's side."

"As he should. I'm going to go outside to sit in the garden for awhile. I think it best I spend some time alone."

I did not wait for either of them to respond, holding back tears that burst forth the moment I stepped out the back side of the castle and into the garden. I sat down on a splintered wooden bench, poorly crafted by my father when he was a young lad. Placing my head in my hands, I wept.

I didn't know for whom I cried, but the tears fell freely. After some time, I felt a strong hand touch my back. I'd been certain I was alone, and I'd heard no one approach. Brushing away tears with my sleeve, I opened my eyes and looked up into the face of Arran.

CHAPTER 38

*A*t first I thought I'd imagined him, that after too many nights of him haunting my dreams, he had now come to torture me while awake, as well. I leapt out of his grasp, staring, open-mouthed, as he gazed at me.

"Blaire, why are ye crying, lass?"

He moved forward to touch me, but I jerked away from him. "Doona touch me. Ye should not be here, Arran. Is it not true what I just heard about Edana and yer child?"

"Nay, only part of what ye heard was true. I'm here to tell ye the rest and to make sure that ye do not marry Baodan. Now tell me, why are ye crying?"

"Ye ask that as if I have naught to cry over." I could not choose just one reason for my tears, for there were many. I was heartbroken for Arran's loss, heartbroken for myself, and angry that he would choose now to reappear in my life.

"Ye doona have reason to wed my cousin anymore, lass. Now that Edana is gone, I am no longer married. Do not marry Baodan. Marry me, as ye are meant to."

Feelings of heartbreak disappeared. Disgust filled me at Arran's callousness over the death of his wife. I'd known that living with her would not be easy for him, but he was a man quite changed from the Arran I had once known and loved. "How can ye speak to me so when she has not been dead a week? I know that ye did not love her, but ye disrespect us both by speaking of her so now. Did ye think I would rejoice over her death and claim ye as my own?"

His brows pulled together, and I could see he was struggling with his words. "Forgive me, lass. I do not mean to sound so cold-hearted, but believe me there are things that ye do not know. Things that I wish to tell ye now. Ye know me well. I have no way about me with the right saying of words."

He sat down where he'd found me and motioned for me to do the same. Hesitantly, I did so, keeping some distance between us, for I knew all too well the power his touch wielded over me. "Then tell it, but I will not marry ye, Arran. I have promised myself to Baodan, and I shall marry him tomorrow."

He shook his head, unbothered by my words. "Nay, ye will do no such thing, lass. If I have to bind ye and carry ye off from here myself, I will do so. Ye will not be marrying anyone save me."

I did not know what to say to that. Part of me wanted to kiss him and tell him how much I'd missed him, while the other part of me wanted to hit him over the head with something large and heavy. I decided, instead, to stay silent and listen to what he had to tell me.

It did not take him long to oblige. "Again, lass, forgive me for sounding cold about Edana's death, but she was a wretched woman, and I canna claim that I am not glad to be free of her. She lied to me, lass. She was never carrying my child."

"Then how did she die?" Twas small relief to know Arran had not lost a child, but I knew that if he'd believed a child was coming, he would be pained to learn that one was not.

"I do not know for sure, lass, but I know that it was no fault of my own. I should not have married her, and I'll regret any pain I caused her always, but I will not be so foolish twice."

I reached out and patted his hand, only allowing my touch to linger for a moment. If this had been all, I would have followed him into marriage this very night, but that was not the case. Part of me was unwilling to forgive him. "I'm so sorry, Arran."

"Sorry for what, lass?"

"I'm sorry that my leaving caused ye to marry her. I'm sorry that she died. And I am sorry, but I cannot marry ye now."

As before, he seemed unconcerned with my denial of him. "Ach, lass, I know that ye do not wish to hurt Baodan, but he is a strong lad. He will find the lass that is meant for him. But ye, Blaire . . . ye are meant for me alone."

I stood and moved away from him, tears threatening once more. "Aye, once that was true, Arran. But Baodan is a better man than ye, and he was there for me when I needed him, when ye refused to come, although I lay dying."

"Dying? I know naught what ye speak of, lass."

He was lying, I was sure of it. But the pained expression on his face did not seem feigned. "How can ye say that ye do not know, Arran? I sent ye a letter when I believed I had only days to live. Bri spoke to the messenger that delivered it straight into yer hands."

He moved too quickly for me to evade him. Grabbing both of my hands into his own, he pleaded, "Believe me, lass, this messenger did not tell Bri the truth. Had I known that ye might die, no matter the cause, there is naught in this world that would keep me from ye. Tell me that ye believe me, Blaire. Ye possess every bit of my heart and soul. Had ye died, I would have, as well. I will not wait to have ye as my wife a moment more."

He kissed me then, and I returned it before moving my lips to his ear so that I could whisper to him. "Aye, I believe ye. It hurt me more than I care to tell ye when I thought that ye knew and did not wish to come."

"Ach, lass. . . "

He sighed heavily into my ear, his breath shaky. I could feel how much he longed for me. Pulling away slightly, he kissed me gently on the lips as he stared into my eyes. In his gaze, I saw everything I'd ever wanted to hear from him. His eyes said more than words ever could.

"It pains me to know that ye could think it of me, but I know that I havena treated ye as I should," he said quietly. "If ye will have me, lass, I shall spend the rest of my life making it up to ye."

"Aye, Arran, I'll marry ye." I kissed him briefly, moaning as his hand on my lower back pulled me to him.

Suddenly, a voice to my left caused us both to grow still. "Will ye, lass? I doona believe that my wedding day will turn out as I'd hoped."

I turned to see Baodan standing close by. While his face gave none of his emotions away, his eyes, deep brown and beautiful, were sad. My heart filled with guilt as it broke for him.

CHAPTER 39

*A*rran left us, understanding that I needed a moment alone with Baodan to explain the best I could what had taken place since we'd last seen each other. I could not tell if he was angry; Baodan was a man whose face was impenetrable. I sensed, though, that even if he was angry, it would take much to get him to express it.

"Baodan, I believe I need to tell you what's happened . . . " My words sounded foolish and obvious, but I knew not what to say. My face felt flushed with heat from my embarrassment and shame.

He surprised me by reaching for my hand, then he led me through the small garden, the two of us walking side-by-side.

"Nay, lass. I doona think ye have as much to explain as ye think ye do."

"What do ye mean?" I allowed him to lead me as we slowly made our way out of the garden, meandering through the castle grounds in the moonlight.

"He is the one, is he not, lass? The one who laid claim over yer heart even when he was no longer with ye? I knew it was my cousin, lass. As I said, ye spoke his name many times when ye were delirious with fever."

"Aye, and I'm so verra sorry, Baodan. I would not have agreed to marry ye if I believed there was any way for Arran and me to be together. But now that there is, I cannot marry ye. It would not be fair to ye for me to do so."

"Aye, I know that ye cannot, lass. I wouldna wish for ye to."

I stopped walking so that he would stop, as well. Facing him, I clasped hold of his other hand. "Truly? Ye are not angry with me?"

He smiled, squeezing my hands gently. "Nay, lass. I am sad that I shall not share in the pleasure of yer company. I think that we could have been bonny friends, aye? But I cannot be angry with ye for doing as yer heart bids. Ye are lucky, lass. Ye have been given the chance to be with the one ye thought ye'd lost. If I was given the same opportunity, not even the fiery pits of hell could stop me. I am happy for ye, Blaire."

I had not expected such a reaction, but after listening to him, I was not surprised. Baodan was the best of men. If I had more brains than heart, I would have married him rather than Arran. I stretched, having to stand on the farthest tips of my toes to reach him and kiss him on the lips. Then I pulled him into a hug. He squeezed me tightly, and my feet came off the ground. Together we stayed there for only a moment.

Once he set me back on the ground, I stepped away from him to walk back to the castle, but I turned to bid him one last farewell. "Goodbye, Baodan. Ye are a good man. There is someone else out there who ye will find, and she will heal yer heart. I have no doubt of it, and there is no man more deserving of finding true love again than ye."

He shook his head shyly. "Nay, lass, I doona know about that. If such a time comes, I shall welcome it, but I will not expect it as I journey forward."

I turned away and went in search of Bri, Mary, and Adelle, silently throwing a prayer up to the heavens that love would find Baodan again. I knew the women in my life would not be pleased with me if I kept all that had happened from them for very long.

---

*P*ure commotion filled the castle by the time I made my way back. Eoin, Mary, Bri, and Adelle were thrilled to see Arran. They were also all ready to resurrect Edana and bury her again after learning of the lies she'd told him. Baodan's family members were so angry with Arran and me over my cancelled wedding to Baodan that I feared a brawl might erupt. Thank goodness Baodan showed up shortly after I arrived and calmed them down, taking them away so they could make their preparations to return home.

As the chaos ensued around me, only one person's reaction concerned me. I searched for my father, and found him leaning casually against a doorway, observing the screaming spectacle with ornery amusement.

He smiled as he spotted me, then quickly made his way over, pulling me into a side corridor before I could be swept away by the flurry of activity in the main hall. "So, I hear that ye've changed yer mind on another wedding, have ye, lass? Please tell me that this one to Arran shall be yer last, and that ye will truly marry him."

I laughed into his chest as I hugged him. "Aye, Father. If I do not, I shall let ye send me away to a convent."

"Doona tempt me, love. Now, let us leave this place. The two of ye can be married at the top of the river near here. It runs into a deep valley and is the prettiest place in all of Scotland. Yer mother and I were married there. If we leave now, we can make it by morning."

We set out in the middle of the night—my father and I on our own horses and Arran and Adelle atop another. She was not an excellent rider, but she was no novice, either. When Arran told her she could ride with him if she wished, she'd wasted no time in accepting his offer. I had a feeling her decision had more to do with her desire to be close to my handsome husband-to-be than her not wanting to ride alone, but it did not bother me a bit. How could I blame her? Her infatuation with handsome men made me smile. And I was secure in the fact that I, and I alone, would be the lucky woman to share Arran's bed from this night onward.

---

*B*y the time we arrived at the river, the sun was just beginning to rise, casting beautiful shades of pink and yellow across the shimmering water that gently trickled down the valley, slicing beautiful curves in the green landscape.

The ceremony was short and simple, rather unlike the pathways we took to reach the spot my father had chosen. Adelle cried loudly throughout our exchange of vows, garnering multiple looks of horror from my father. But at the ceremony's completion as we sealed the vows with a kiss, I didn't miss the small trickle of tears that fell from Father's eyes, as well.

Arran pulled me in close, running his fingers deep into my hair as he placed a trail of tiny kisses up to my ear. "I dinna think I would ever be able to call ye wife, but in my heart I always thought of ye as such."

I shifted my head and brought my lips toward his once more. Quickly saying our farewells, we left Father and Adelle to make their way back to MacChristy Castle alone. Mounting Arran's horse together, we set off down the valley, not knowing what direction we sought and not caring, as long as we were headed there together. . . and alone.

CHAPTER 40

ormod waited until the group had split in two and each had departed – Arran and Blaire off toward the north, and Laird MacChristy and an unfamiliar lass riding back toward MacChristy Castle. Only then did he crawl from his hiding space and walk far off to the west where he'd left his horse tied to a tree.

Immediately after Edana's death, Tormod had gone into the village to spend time in the ale house, hoping that he would be able to spread suspicion of how Edana had met her death among the townspeople. His efforts had been fruitless.

Everyone he spoke to had lived under the miserable leadership of Ramsay Kinnaird and were not as sympathetic as he'd hoped toward Edana and her untimely fate. Most were also suspicious of him. Wretched man or not, Ramsay's blood pumped through him. Knowing this, the townspeople were unlikely to trust him unless given real reason.

The people saw Arran and all of the Conalls as saviors who had finally delivered them from the all-powerful hold of his uncle. It had only taken him upsetting a small handful of villagers before he'd been run out of the ale house. They would not allow him to speak ill of their new laird or suggest that he'd done something so heinous.

Arran hadn't, of course, but the truth of Edana's death could never be known if Tormod was to ever take over as laird. He had left the ale house angry and defeated. The next few days were spent sulking, until he saw Arran ride from their territory in the direction of Conall Castle.

It didn't take him long to guess where or to whom Arran was riding. Tormod knew he was travelling to see his lover, anxious to fall into her arms now that he was rid of his wife. Not that he could blame him. There was no denying that the lass was a great beauty.

Tormod knew not how Arran's new marriage to Blaire could contribute to his downfall, but he was sure that once he told his sister, she could figure out a way to turn it to their favor. He rode quickly, anxious to arrive home so a plan could be made and a trap set before Arran and his new bride returned to their stolen castle.

"Ye are certain they are married? He dinna just take her to his bed?"

Tormod ground his teeth in frustration. She was smarter than he, but he was no fool. Fia often spoke to him as if he were a small child, not the man who would soon serve as her laird. "Aye, I would not have ridden so fast to ye if I was not absolutely certain. I saw it with my own two eyes."

"Aye, good. Ye shall use his new bride to turn the people against him."

"How? The people doona wish to hear talk against him, especially if it should come from either of us."

"Aye, 'twas foolish of ye to try and sway anyone yerself to begin with. All we need is to pay someone else to do our bidding as we did before. The people are too loyal to Arran and the Conalls, but they have not had as much interaction with the MacChristys. It will be easier for them to believe ill of Blaire if the news comes from someone that lives among them and they accept as part of the village. We are outsiders, ye and I. Go and gather the midwife who confirmed Edana's lie to Arran. If she is not willing to help us, take her children."

ormod reared back to kick in the door of Gara's home with as much force as he could muster. The small wooden shack was dark, and he hoped to scare Gara and her family out of their beds. When the lass saw him with his lit torch, ready to set her home ablaze, she would come with him willingly, and he would not be forced to take her beastly children.

He moved throughout the small space, holding his torch in front of him, slowly realizing the shack was empty. Not only were Gara and her children not there, it was evident by the lack of personal belongings that they never planned to return.

Perhaps the lass had more brains than he'd realized. She'd not taken his threats idly. Still, he knew that his sister would not be pleased to know that they no longer had Gara under their control. But tonight was not the night for her to upset him. Tormod was itching for violence. One day his sister would push him too far.

"*W*hat do ye mean, she is not there? God, how could ye be so daft, Tormod? To let her go after what she knows? I told ye we should have disposed of her after she served her purpose the first time."

Tormod threw his fist hard against the doorway, his frustration at his sister reaching a point where he was afraid he could no longer control his anger. "Are ye not the one who suggested that we go to the lass and enlist her service now? I am tired of ye speaking to me as ye do! Ye doona know to whom ye speak. Soon, I will be laird of this territory. If ye doona wish to stay in the ruins in which we live now, you willna speak to me so ever again."

He blanched when she slapped him hard across the face, and his fists began to tremble as the world around him disappeared. All he could see was her screaming. He knew not what she said, only making out an occasional word that escaped her vile mouth as rage filled him. There had been too many years of her belittling him, of her ordering him about and behaving as if he was useless without her.

Fia might have been quicker to think of ideas, but Tormod always followed them through. Suddenly he knew how to bring down Arran. All he had to do was find another castle servant he could coerce to do his bidding. He had no further need for his sister.

"Doona ye threaten me," Fia hissed. "Ye're a fool. Ye were born a fool, and a fool ye shall stay. Any triumph that ye have ever seen has been owed to me. Ye are as useless as our horrid father and as daft as our mother."

As quickly as Tormod's rage had risen, an eerie sense of calm replaced it. Suddenly, it was all clear to him. Fia was no more than an obstacle, one that he could no longer allow to stand in his way.

"Goodbye, sister." He reached forward, ramming her head hard against the doorway. She was knocked unconscious at once, and when Tormod felt for a pulse, there was none.

He stepped over her lifeless body and made his way to the castle. It would be easy to find someone willing to do his bidding, and if they would not, they would meet the same fate as Edana and his sister.

CHAPTER 41

*A*rran and I rode casually, not making haste to anywhere as we followed the river deeper into the valley. We were both as happy as we'd ever been, but equally as exhausted. Arran, especially, had gone days without sleep, and I could hear his soft snoring against my ear as I rode in front of him on the horse.

I laughed quietly, just loud enough to wake him and send him jerking upright in the saddle.

"I think 'tis time for us to take a rest, aye? If ye start to topple off the horse, I will not be able to keep ye from falling." I leaned back and turned my head to kiss him as he pulled up on the reins to slow the horse's pace.

Dismounting, he tied the horse to a tree. Hand-in-hand, we made our way to the river. After searching for a few moments, we found the softest patch of earth and lay next to each other to rest our eyes for awhile.

I curled into the nook of his arm, imagining that while we intended to sleep, Arran would first suggest that we partake of another enjoyable activity. But no sooner had I settled myself comfortably next to him than he was snoring loudly.

I reached up, lightly kissing his brow before I rested my head against him to try and sleep awhile myself, but I dinna drift long before I grew restless and stood to stretch. I would let him sleep as long as he needed. It was a beautiful summer day, and I'd taken a fancy to sticking my feet into the running stream so I could feel the water swish between my toes. My last experience with water briefly crossed my mind, but I dinna fear the river with Arran by my side.

The water was cold, but it felt nice in contrast to the warm sun that beat down on my face. I leaned back, extending my neck to spread the warmth over me. I knew not how long I lay there, but I heard Arran approaching before I felt his hands on my shoulders.

"Ach, lass, ye look beautiful with yer bare feet splashing in the water and yer bare neck red from the sun. If I wasna a gentleman, I would take ye right here."

"Gentleman? Ha! Where might my husband be? I know not of this gentleman that ye speak of." I kept my back to him, smiling as he sat behind me. His arms wrapped around my waist and he laced his fingers together, leaning in to lightly blow warm air into my ear and down my back.

I laughed at the sensation, squirming as he held me tight, tickling me with his warm breath.

We went still after a time, and I turned my head to kiss him, but nipped his earlobe, instead.

I smiled as I heard his breath catch. He had not expected me to tease him so.

"Oh, do ye not know what that does to me, lass? Doona tempt me," he crooned in my ear. "I do not wish to treat ye like an animal and have ye in the middle of nature for any passerby to see. But if ye continue, I may lose all sense of restraint."

I wiggled closer against him, turned my head again, and stuck my tongue in his ear, intending to torture him so that he would change his mind. "I do not care if anyone sees. But look around, I think we are all alone save for the birds and fishes."

He disappointed me by bending his knees so that he could jump to his feet. "Nay, lass. Ye are my wife. I want to honor ye in a bed with a roof above us. I willna take ye until we have found shelter for the night."

I raised my toes out of the water, shaking them dry. Then I stood quickly making my way back to the horse. "Let's ride then, and I do not wish to make as slow go of it as we did this morning. I am not a patient lass, husband, and I'm anxious for this honoring that ye speak of. Where shall we stay this evening?"

He smiled, following suit as we made our way to the horse, him mounting first and then assisting me so that I sat in front of him, mimicking our positions by the river. "There is a small village nay far from here, and there is an inn where we will stay for the night. 'Tis a common place of rest for travelers so they doona often have rooms, but my father knew the owners well. They shall have a room for us, I am certain."

"Sounds lovely."

"Aye, lass. Lovely is too tame a word for what I have in mind."

"'Tis some promise ye make, lad," I teased. "I hope ye are up to the task." I smiled, squealing as he released the reins with one of his hands and gently pinched my bottom.

"Do ye doubt it, lass? Well, I shall prove ye wrong soon enough."

---

*A*rran was not a liar. After giving the old couple who owned the inn a generous number of coins, we were provided a comfortable room at the farthest corner of the establishment. He'd certainly intended to assure that we would not be disturbed for the evening.

We had waited much too long for this moment, and for most of that time, we thought it would never arrive. I always imagined that I would be nervous my first time, but I was not. As we lay side-by-side across the bed, facing one another, our eyes locked, and Arran stroking my hair, my longing for him left no room for nerves. He was my love, my husband, my life. We had overcome many obstacles, and I had crossed time and come back again so we could be one. For me, it could not happen too soon.

He sent me a mischievous smile and I returned it with one of my own. "Before we arrived," I said in a teasing tone, twirling a strand of his golden hair around my finger, "I seem to recall ye mentioned honoring me, aye?"

"Aye, and I seem to recall ye doubted me being up to the task," he said in a tone that mimicked mine. "I'll have ye know, I have been with many women, lass, and I know what each one of them desires."

I stiffened, not liking the direction he'd taken the conversation. I'd always known that, though he was mine, I would not be his first. Still, I did not wish to be reminded. "If ye wish to honor me, mayhap it would be best for ye not to tell me just how many women ye have treated thus. It does nothing to make me feel special, aye?"

He placed one finger across my lips to silence me. "Hush, lass. Ye dinna let me finish. I know what they want, but I have never given it to any of them."

"Ye are too sure of yerself, Arran. How can ye know what all women want?"

"What they want, lass, is to be worshiped, for a man to surrender himself to them, giving them his soul so that he will nay love another for the rest of his days." He kissed me thoroughly before adding, "It has been asked of me many times in the way a lass would touch me, opening her heart, begging me to give her that most precious part of myself. But I always tucked it away, never understanding why I couldna let that part of myself go. Now I know."

"Aye?" My heart fluttered so wildly in my chest, the word came out of me breathlessly.

"Aye, lass. 'Twas for ye. My heart waited for ye before I knew ye were to come into my life. I shall worship ye now, love, and as I do so, know that I share with ye my soul, for there is no other in my life but ye. For the truth is, lass, that ye've possessed my soul since the first time I saw ye. By the end of this night, I shall lay claim over yers, as well."

"Oh, Arran, do ye not know by now that ye already do?"

"Ye are my first love, Blaire. My first and my last," he said then, his voice a deep caress in my ear.

"And ye are mine," I whispered, as tears of joy filled my eyes. "I will never let anything keep us apart again."

"Nor will I."

The night faded away around us, and for me there was only Arran. His eyes, his warmth, his whisper of my name. All mine, this night and forever more.

CHAPTER 42

"Now what did I tell ye, man?" Tormod stepped away, releasing the old man who'd served as gardener at the castle for three generations of Kinnairds, allowing him the chance to speak as he'd bid him.

"If I doona do what ye ask, ye shall kill my wife. Ye have her locked away and gagged where I canna get to her."

Tormod groaned at the trembling man. "Nay, ye fool. I shall certainly do all that ye have said, but I intended for ye to tell me what ye are to say to the villagers after ye gather them together this evening. Are ye certain they will come if ye send for them?

He glared at the old man, watching as he reached up to rub the side of his cheek, now red from the impact of his palm. "Aye, sir. I know all in the village and all know me. They shall listen to whatever I have to say to them."

"Good and what is it exactly, man, that ye have to say?"

"That…that Blaire MacChristy is a witch. That I've seen her steal herbs from my garden so she could cast her spells. That I believe she has bewitched Arran for some time, and it was she that killed Edana, not the loss of a child."

"And what will ye tell them of Arran if they should find him innocent in Blaire's wrongdoing?"

"That the spell she cast on him is too strong and has addled his brain such that his bond to her will only be severed by death. That if we are to keep our village and children safe, we must rid ourselves of both Arran and his new bride, the MacChristy witch."

"Aye, man. Now doona ye forget what shall happen to ye if ye should waver in yer story. I will be in the crowd listening to yer every word. If ye should waver, 'tis yer wife that shall suffer."

Tears rolled down the old man's face, and they brightened Tormod's heart. Finally, he was the man he'd always hoped to be. People feared him. If his ancestors had taught him anything, it was that with fear came power.

He sent the man away to gather his clansmen.

---

*W*e spent two more nights at the inn, then started for home, where we hoped for nothing more than to have at least a fortnight of peaceful nothingness.

It took us mere moments as we neared the castle to know that we would not get our wish. It was night, but a large crowd gathered. We heard angry voices while still a good distance from the stables.

"What do ye think has happened, Arran?" Fear gripped me in the belly, and I fought back the urge to beg Arran to turn the horse around so we could flee from here. Something in the back of my mind warned me that the crowd awaited us.

"I doona know, lass, but surely there is need to worry."

His words were meant to comfort me, but tension hardened his body. Even the horse was hesitant to continue marching forward the closer we got to the village.

"I think ye are wrong, Arran. They've spotted us, and some of them are now headed in our direction. Perhaps we should leave."

"Nay, lass. I am laird of this keep now. Whatever has occurred, 'tis my duty to see to it and see that my people are cared for. I'm sure that all they need is leadership to assist in whatever has occurred."

"Aye, I'm sure ye are right." I knew that he was not, but I did not wish to cause him to fear the approaching crowd any more than I knew he already did.

Slowly, we drew closer. As soon as I heard the words the people chanted, my blood ran cold.

"Witch. Witch. Witch." They screamed it over and over, fingers pointing at me while their pity-filled eyes turned toward Arran.

"What is the meaning of this? Who among ye will step forward to tell me what has happened whilst I was away?"

An elderly man standing apart from the crowd hollered out, gesturing wildly at me. "That be her, the witch. We should bind them at once."

I couldn't make sense of what the man said, but I didn't miss the way he cast his eyes downward after he finished speaking, not looking up again as the crowd poured in around us. Two men stepped forward with chains, roughly dragging us off of the horse, chaining us before either of us had time to scream or protest.

Our mouths were gagged and our eyes covered as they led us away to somewhere deep below the castle. Not until we were thrown into cells did they remove our coverings, but it was too dark in the cell for me to see anything. I called out for Arran, feeling frantically around the darkness. "Arran! Arran, where are ye? What has happened?"

A voice that I had not heard before teased me in the darkness.

Malice dripped from the deep, unsettling tone, and I screamed as large hands gripped me hard by both arms.

"Arran is not here, lass, and I doona think that ye shall ever see him again."

CHAPTER 43

"There is no need for ye to do this, sister. Yer children need ye, and ye shall all be safe here if ye will only agree to stay."

Gara pulled her sister into a large embrace but shook her head, resigned to the decision she knew she must make. "Nay, I canna continue to live with the wrong that I've done. I lied once to provide for my children, and it resulted in the death of a lass who'd seen naught but heartache her whole life. I lied once more to protect them, but I canna be the mother they deserve if I am not willing to do what is right."

"But ye doona know for certain what Tormod plans. Why do ye think ye shall be able to stop it?"

Gara didn't respond right away, squatting so that she could kiss each of her three children, holding them tight as she prayed it wouldn't be the last time she got to hold them in her arms.

"Go inside my dear ones, and be good for yer auntie whilst I am away. I love ye more than ye shall ever know."

She controlled her sobs until the children were inside her sister's home. Struggling to catch her breath, she gasped, "I doona know what I shall do, but I know that I must try. I heard

Tormod in the ale house doing his best to make the men believe that Arran killed Edana. He did no such thing, but Tormod willna rest until he has succeeded in turning my people against them. 'Tis time that I share the truth with my clansmen."

"But ye must know that he shall kill ye if ye do so," her sister warned.

Gara nodded, pulling her cloak over her so that she could be on her way. "Aye, but I am not living now with the guilt tearing me into pieces. If I should die, at least my soul will be at peace knowing I have made amends for the sin I committed."

"God go with ye, sister."

Gara turned, fleeing into the night so she would not be tempted to turn back and live as a coward. She could only hope that one day her children would know of her bravery and grow up to be the men and women she'd given her life to allow them to be.

---

*A*rran would not allow himself to lose Blaire again. If he had to break his own legs and ribs to get out of his cell, he would find a way to save her. Any man that got in his way would find himself dead, clansman or not.

He rammed his shoulder hard against the metal. If only he could get one of the bars loose, he could somehow squeeze his way out. It was so dark he could scarcely see, but a noise at the end of the hallway alerted him that he was no longer alone. He stilled instantly, patting himself down for anything he could use as a weapon.

"Sir, are ye there? Tis Gara."

He could think of no reason for her to be down here. His first thought was that she must have been one of the ones to conspire against him. He knew that she'd already lied to him at least once before. Had she lied again when she said she knew nothing else?

But on second thought, he remembered that she'd come to him, risking her own safety to tell him the truth of Edana's lie about the child.

He called out to her, doing his best to be loud enough so she could hear him, but restraining somewhat so he would not draw attention from elsewhere in the dungeon. "Aye, lass. Do ye know why I was placed here?"

He listened as she made her way toward him. When she stepped into the small beam of moonlight streaming into his cell, he saw fear on her face and knew that she was not there to harm him.

"Aye. Tormod has convinced everyone that the lass ye are with is a witch, and she killed Edana. He says she has ye under a mighty spell."

Anger boiled inside of Arran. He'd wanted to kill Tormod the moment he'd first laid eyes on him, able to see the lad's evil spirit through the hatred that shone in his eyes.

"Why would he do it? What does he have to gain from it?" Arran believed he knew the answer, but it was hard for him to imagine anyone wanting to be laird enough to go to such lengths. Ruling a keep was hard work, and if he could go back, he would gladly give up his position as laird, but not to a man like Tormod.

"He wishes to be laird. He believes it is his right because he is the bastard son of Ramsay's brother."

"Do ye know where they've taken Blaire? What does he intend to do to her?" His heart beat quickly at the thought of Blaire being harmed. If Tormod hurt her in any way, Arran would return whatever pain he inflicted on her, tenfold.

"Nay, sir. I doona know where she is, but the clansmen intend to kill her. That is clear from the mob that awaits ye outside."

Arran beat his fist hard against the stone wall, growling at the pain. "I am not so worried about the mob. All I can think of now is Blaire. I must get to her before Tormod causes her harm."

The woman blinked troubled eyes at him. "I dinna tell ye the whole truth last time I spoke to ye. I was too afraid that Tormod would hurt my children, but now I have seen them safely away to be with my sister, and I have come to right the wrongs I have played a part in."

"What is it, lass? What dinna ye tell me last time we spoke?"

"Edana dinna die naturally. Poison killed her. A poison Tormod instructed her to take. I doona believe that she knew it would kill her. I believe she thought it would only mimic an early birth and the loss of a child."

Arran shook his head in the darkness, disgust rising in the form of bile in the back of his throat. "How could anyone be so evil? Do ye know of a way to get out of here, lass? 'Tis urgent that I do so before Tormod can cause harm to anyone else."

"Aye, sir. I have worked in the castle most of my life, and I know where a set of keys is kept hidden. I've fetched them for you."

Arran breathed a deep sigh of relief as he watched Gara pull the keys out from under her dress and begin to work on his lock. Once he was free, he pulled her into a quick embrace, then departed in the direction of the other cell block.

CHAPTER 44

I dinna know the man who held on tightly to me in the darkness. He pushed me back hard into the cell wall and growled a sound so inhuman that the evil in it caused me to shiver uncontrollably. I was certain that my life was about to end.

A sound in the distance caused him to pull away from me, and I had to swallow to keep from emptying my stomach onto the cell floor.

"I did as ye bid me. Now, tell me where I can find my wife."

The voice sounded old and frightened, and I knew that whatever he asked of the creature next to me, he would not receive what he hoped for.

The stranger spoke, calling the man to approach him. "Come here, gardener, and I shall tell ye where ye can find yer wife."

My eyes slowly opened themselves to the darkness, and I could see the outline of the old man as he approached the cell. I also saw a glint of metal as my captor pulled a knife from his boot. I charged him, jumping on his back and bringing my fist down on the top of his head with as much strength as I could muster.

The beast was too strong. While it caused him to shift his arm so that his blow to the man wasna fatal, the dirk still slipped easily into the old man's side. I screamed loudly, hoping for anyone to hear me and come to my aid, for I knew that the dirk would be headed for me next.

My captor was on me in an instant, grabbing my throat with one hand and pinning both of my wrists above my head with the other. I could hear footsteps headed in our direction, but it didn't seem the choker could make out the sound. His face contorted with rage as he did his best to squeeze the life out of me.

He was succeeding. As my vision faded, I was unsure if it was truly Arran that I saw reach to grab the dagger out of the man's side, then charge through the open cell to send the weapon deep into my assailant's neck.

The monster's hold on me instantly released, and I sank to my knees, desperate to catch a breath as the blood from the man's neck continued to spray over me. I retched at the taste of it dripping into my mouth, and I stepped away, not wishing to be near him as he took his last breath.

His eyes remained open, the same evil expression forever plastered on his face. Even in death, the beast beneath the man shone through.

It took me a moment to catch my breath. By the time my head cleared, I could see Arran and a woman I didn't know bent over the elderly man who gasped painfully at the knife wound in his side.

"Doona worry, lad. We shall get ye the care that ye need. Only hold on a moment more, and we shall find someone to tend to ye."

I watched as the man reached out to grab Arran's arm, preventing him from going for help. "Nay, lad. If ye leave here before the clan knows the truth, they shall murder ye on the spot. I am not long for this world, and I doona wish to be, either. I understand now that Tormod killed my wife before I even agreed to do as he asked. There is no place in this world for me if she is not here at my side."

Arran shook his head, intent on helping the man. "Nay, lad. Ye shall live many years still."

The woman on his other side shook her head, interrupting him. "I'm verra sorry, but ye are wrong, sir. The old man is right. He has only a few moments left, and there is naught that we can do to help him."

I dinna know the elder, but tears sprang up in my eyes. If he hadna arrived when he had, it would be me lying on the cell floor dead. This man had saved my life.

"Aye, I told ye, lad. I know that I am dying, and I doona wish for it to be any other way. At least help me to fix the wrong I've done to ye. Ye and yer lady must stay hidden until the people have heard what I have to say. Gara, will ye help me to my feet and let me lean against ye so that, together, we can address them? Once we have both spoken, ye will be free to leave here, and I will die knowing that I dinna let the monster win."

I could see that Arran knew he would not change the old man's mind. He rose from his knees, pulling the man up with him so that he could situate him on Gara's shoulders. He helped them to the doorway. Then, sending them out on their own, he returned to my side.

"God, lass, I thought I had lost ye."

"And I ye." I threw myself into his arms, sobbing as he reached to wipe the blood from my face.

A sudden hush outside the dungeon told us that our saviors now had the attention of the crowd. Hand-in-hand, we moved to the doorway and hid in the shadows as we watched them inform the crowd of all Tormod's evildoings.

The clansmen did not seem surprised. Once the truth was known, the crowd gathered in close around the gardener, no longer in anger but to comfort their friend as he took his last breaths.

Arran and I remained hidden in the shadows as the clansmen left the village to grieve their friend and hero. Gara came to us as they carried the old man's body away to prepare for burial. Relief etched her face. I could tell then that she'd risked her own life for us, as well, not knowing if she would come out of it alive.

"Thank ye, Gara. We owe ye a debt that we can never repay." Arran clasped the woman's shoulder, unsure of how to express his gratitude.

"Ye owe me nothing. I am more fortunate than I thought possible. My conscience is now clear of the wrong I did ye, and I will return to my children when I dinna believe I would ever be able to do so. If ye follow this pathway through the dungeon, it will lead ye back into the castle where ye can clean yerselves up and rest, away from everyone. Now, excuse me, I have bairns that I need to gather in my arms."

Once she was gone, we silently made our way through the dungeons, not stopping until we were inside the castle. We knew that we would not sleep, despite our fatigue. We were both eager to await the sun, for it was the only way this day would truly feel over.

CHAPTER 45

"Are ye sure that ye are fine with this, Arran?" I asked. "For if this is something that ye want, I will stand by yer side. I know there are many dark memories in this place, but I believe that we could make new ones here." I walked up behind him as he finished penning his letter that detailed to his clansmen why he was to step down as laird.

"Aye, lass, I doona doubt that we could, but I doona wish to. This is not our home, and these people are not our people."

"They did accept you at first, did they not?"

He twisted in his seat, wrapping his arms around me as he buried his head in my breasts. "Aye, lass, they did, but they turned on me rather quickly, as well. I dinna wish to be laird to begin with. I rushed into it foolhardily because I believed that I was helping another. If only I could have seen all the trouble that decision would cause us."

I kissed the top of his head. "There is no sense in thinking that way. No one can know just where their decisions will take them. All we can do now is make the best of our future."

"Is this decision pleasing to ye as well, lass? I wish to please ye and, if ye wish to stay, I shall."

I shook my head, unable to repress the shiver that traveled through me at the thought. He squeezed me tightly in understanding. "Nay, I doona wish to stay. I wish to return to Conall Castle to live in the happy chaos with yer brother, Mary, Bri, and Adelle. And then, when it is time that my father can no longer serve as laird, ye can replace him. But for now, let us live more simply, with none of the responsibilities and troubles that come with a lairdship."

Arran stood, sealing his letter and slipping it away to give to Gara. She would be sure to share it with the clan, who in time would find a laird from within their own group of men.

The people would not be surprised to learn of our decision to leave. Few would approach us still, their guilt from their accusations toward us making them hesitant to speak.

"Ach, lass, ye are a mind reader, I'm sure, for there is nothing that I wish to do more than all that ye have just said. Come, let us leave this place."

---

*A*rran was not deserving of the blessings given to him, of nothing he'd ever been more certain. Many men better than he were more deserving of Blaire and her love, but he would gladly spend the rest of his life trying to make himself worthy of her.

She'd healed him from a broken spirit, forgiven him of his wrongs again and again, and shown him the value that comes with finding someone with whom to share all of life's struggles.

He leaned forward to smell her hair as she rode before him, stunned by how just her scent alone could elicit emotions in him he'd never known existed before. He couldn't wait to give her a babe—a son or a daughter with eyes just like their mother's. As soon as they returned to Conall Castle, he planned to immediately begin work on that task.

Or mayhap, even better, he would begin tonight as they stopped at the McMillans' to rest on their journey home.

———

*W*e took the long route back to Conall Castle and, much to my dismay, Arran insisted that we stop at the McMillans' on our way home. Baodan was Arran's favorite cousin, and he'd not had the chance to make peace with him the night Baodan found us together in the garden.

'Twas not Baodan I worried about seeing, but I knew that his mother wouldna welcome me with open arms. By a happy coincidence, she was away when we arrived. It allowed us to spend a pleasant evening with Baodan and his brothers, all of whom I was certain would become my dear friends.

The next morning we set off early, determined to make it back to Conall Castle within two more nights. I'd settled comfortably in my seat in front of Arran, nearly falling asleep as I leaned back against his shoulder, when an odd flash of red caught my attention out of the corner of my eye.

I sat up so quickly, my heels unintentionally went hard into the side of the horse, and Arran had to pull hard at the reins to get the beast back under control. "What is it, lass? Ye nearly scared the poor animal to death."

"Did ye not see that woman, Arran? In the pond?"

Arran pulled back so that the horse came to a stop, and he twisted to look back on the pond that sat just at the edge of McMillan Castle. "Nay, lass, I doona see anyone. Ye saw a woman, ye say? Perhaps, someone is only taking a dip. The morning's nice enough for it, would ye not agree?"

I shook my head; the notion was mad. "Nevermind. I must have dozed for a moment and dreamed something strange."

Arran slowly nudged the horse forward. "Nay, lass. Ye were not asleep; I can always tell by yer breathing when ye are. Tell me. Who do ye think ye saw?"

"The woman looked just like a lass I met in the twenty-first century. A dear friend of Bri's."

"Aye? Well, I will tell ye that does sound mighty strange, but tis not so impossible, either."

He was kind enough not to call me mad, but I wasna eager to discuss it with him further. "Aye, 'tis strange. Doona mind me, I am only overtired." I nudged him playfully in the ribs.

He laughed into my ear, and I smiled, the imaginary figure quickly disappearing from my mind as he kissed the back of my head and tightened his grip around me. We rode toward Conall Castle—to our home—where we would finally be able to build a future together.

EPILOGUE

The Roadside Inn – Present Day

"Jerry, 'tis time for us to make ready once more." Morna stood, stretching after her dream as she smiled wide. It would be fun to tweak her spells, and necessary if the new lass were to cross paths with the one she was meant to.

"O'course, love. What have ye seen?"

"We need to make our home visible once more, but it shall be different from the times before. The redhead is coming our way." She smiled, knowing Jerry would be pleased. He loved company, and he'd taken a liking to the fiery lass who'd come so valiantly in search of her friend.

"Ah, 'tis verra good news, but why should this be different? Do ye not think the lass will stumble across the spell on her own? Bri and Blaire managed quite nicely."

Morna shook her head. It was unlike any dream she'd had before, but she was certain as to its meaning. "Nay, 'tis not that.

The lass will find the spell, but she canna use the same one that's been used before. For while my spell room shall be her portal, it doesna need to be her destination."

"How do ye know?"

"Because one of our lassies has already caught sight of the lass elsewhere, even before she's actually arrived. It seems that a force more powerful than myself sees fit to warn the Conalls of the girl's arrival."

---

*T*urn the page for a Sneak Peek of *Morna's Magic*, Book 3 of The Magical Matchmaker's Legacy.

SNEAK PEEK OF MORNA'S MAGIC - BOOK 3

CHAPTER 1

Austin, TX—Present Day

Two thoughts flashed through my mind as my trembling fingers gripped at the letter and the set of keys my husband held out to me. The first was that if Brian said one more word, I planned to take off my shoe and ram the pointy end of the heel deep into his skull. The second was that I was so ashamed of my own stupidity that I was just as inclined to ram the heel of the other shoe into my own head.

How could I have let so many months pass with him making the most ridiculous excuses to stay away from home? How could I not have caught on? What a silly, desperate fool I must be to have made it so easy for him to break his vows. It must've thrilled him to discover he'd married such an unassuming, trusting wife.

Now that I knew what he'd been up to, over a year's worth of clues seemed glaringly obvious. While we'd never truly been happy, I never thought him capable of such a betrayal. He was an ass, but a cheat? A liar? I'd not seen this in him.

I'd had plenty of time to come to terms with his affair. Weeks of lawyer negotiations and packing my belongings had quickly made me glad to be rid of him. But what had me shaking with anger and unshed tears was the revelation I held in my hand.

"Are you really so surprised, Mitsy?" Brian said defensively. "Bri left too quickly to sell the place, and it's not like she had that many friends. She left it in your care so why shouldn't I have used her house? What did it hurt?"

I squeezed the key so tightly that its ridges buried deep into my hand, indenting the skin. I was sure he could see the steam coming out of my ears, but I refused to scream at him as he expected me to. Brian would call it another one of my "ginger" moments and use it as justification for the affair. I would not give him the satisfaction.

"No." I said the word calmly and slowly released my breath so that it didn't come out as a loud sigh of frustration. "I'm not surprised she left me the house, I'd just never given it much thought. What I'm surprised about is how you thought it was okay to keep this letter from me. This is not addressed to you."

He chuckled, and I ground my heel into the floor to keep myself from ripping it off and attacking him.

"You're right. It isn't, but we were married when it came in the mail and what's yours is mine, yes? Besides, Leah and I needed somewhere to go. It's not like we could come back here when you were always sitting in the house waiting on me."

My face could not have grown any hotter, but still I did not raise my voice. "You can justify anything, can't you? Bri would strangle you herself if she knew you'd been using her house to cheat on me."

Turning from him, I walked across the room to swing the last of my belongings, all thrown messily into a large duffle bag, over my shoulder so that I could make my way out the door. I'd not even read the letter yet. As soon as I saw Bri Conall's handwriting and the key tucked inside the envelope, I knew that my friend had left her house in my care. The date at the top showed just how long Brian had kept this from me.

There was so much more that I could say to him, so much more I wanted to say, but I knew none of it would do any good. He would never see anything wrong with the kind of man he was, and I was tired of him. I was tired of everything, really. I only wanted to get out of this house without saying another word. I didn't ever want to see him again.

"I wasn't the only one who cheated," Brian said behind me. "Maybe you didn't do it physically, but in your mind you did. Every time I held you, I could see *him* behind your eyes. It's too bad for you, really. He didn't want you, either. That's why you ran to me, isn't it?"

I didn't respond. If only Brian would let me be and not say anything else, I might be able to make it out of the room and to my car without bursting into tears. But I knew he wouldn't be so kind.

"Bri is nuts," he continued. "She rambles on in the letter about you coming to visit her at the castle and how much you would love the seventeenth century. Bri's completely out of her mind. No wonder you two were such good friends."

I kept my back to him as I reached for the door handle, and I swallowed the lump in my throat when he chuckled again. "Goodbye, Brian." I didn't look back as I walked out the door, climbed into my car and started the engine, then pulled out of the driveway.

In the rearview mirror I saw Brian's mistress, Leah, pulling into the spot I'd just deserted, replacing me so quickly at our home it was as if I'd never been there. I couldn't bring myself to feel any hatred toward her. Only pity. God help her, the poor girl had no idea what she'd gotten herself into.

As much as I didn't want to spend the night at Bri's old house, especially after learning what Brian had used it for, I was relieved to cancel my hotel reservations. Classroom teachers don't make much money, and as a teacher's aide, I made even less. I couldn't move into my new apartment for another week, and with no family to offer me shelter until then, I had no choice but to reserve a room at the shabbiest of hotels.

If it meant saving a little money, I could push away the memories that would flood over me at Bri's—Brian's love nest. Memories of nights spent with Brian there when it had been his and we'd been dating, before he sold the house to my friend. Memories of helping Bri paint and refurbish the old bachelor pad until it was beautiful and perfect, just as she wished it. It's not as if I planned on sleeping much anyway.

The flowers on the front porch that she once tended so carefully had long since died, and an uncomfortable pang knocked on my heart at the thought of how much I missed Bri. I still didn't fully understand what had happened to her. She was the classroom teacher, and I worked directly under her. She was also the closest friend I'd ever had. When she disappeared after accompanying her archaeologist mother on a dig in Scotland, it's no stretch to say that I lost it a little.

When I finally found her after flying to Scotland, it was clear that she'd fallen madly in love. I saw how much her new husband, Eoin, adored her, and I couldn't blame her a bit for leaving everything behind. I would've done the same.

I'd experienced love like that once, but it hadn't been with

Brian. What he'd said to me was true. The loss of Jep—the man I'd loved—led me to settle for Brian.

I understood Bri when it came to the love thing. What I didn't understand was why she'd lied to me about it. She had lied so confidently, weaving a story so detailed that I truly did want to believe it, but I couldn't. People do not—and she did not—travel through time.

Anxious to read her letter, I turned the key and stepped inside the entryway. To my surprise, the place was immaculate. Well, at least the front part of the house was. Most likely only one area of the house had been regularly used, and I would stay clear of that room.

I dropped my bag in the doorway, carrying only the letter into the living room with me as I slowly made my way around the space, turning on lamps and lighting a few candles.

Once the room was properly lit and the smell of pumpkin-scented candles wafted sweetly through the air, I went into the kitchen and put a kettle of water on the stovetop to heat, preparing to steep a large cup of tea. I was in desperate need of something to soothe my frazzled nerves and angry heart.

It had been weeks since I'd slept properly. Now that the divorce was final and Brian was out of my life, all of the stress, sadness, anxiety, and insomnia of the past weeks seemed to hit me at once.

After the kettle whistled and I poured the steaming water over a large cup filled with several tea bags, I all but collapsed onto the oversized sofa that sat in the middle of the living room. I found a coaster and set my tea cup on it, then propped the pillows up behind me so that I could sit comfortably while reading Bri's letter.

I was incredibly curious to do so. I'd not heard a word from her since the wedding. She'd not even taken the time to say goodbye, slipping away during the middle of the reception. I was still angry about that, but I supposed Bri had her reasons. And she did leave me a house, which certainly counted for something. Not that she could've known just how much I would need it. Or perhaps she had, and that was the very reason she had left it for me. Bri had never really liked Brian.

I didn't need to open the envelope. Brian had already done that, and the rumpled edges showed just how many times he'd read through it himself, clearly trying to make sense of Bri's words.

The letter was short and the handwriting definitely Bri's, although it looked hurried. Something told me her idea to write the letter had been a last minute thought before she returned to Scotland. The first part was what I'd expected—an apology for leaving so suddenly and an explanation that the house was now mine to use as I saw fit. She spoke of how much she loved me, how much my friendship meant to her. Then she launched into what Brian had mentioned, speaking of her love of life in the seventeenth century and suggesting I might love it, too.

After that, she changed subjects quickly, only writing a few sentences at the bottom of the page. She'd not even bothered to sign her name.

"The house is yours while you need it, Mitsy, but when it comes time for you to get away and you're ready to start a new life, come and find me. You're welcome here. You will need the help of the innkeepers you met in Scotland. I'm not going to bother trying to tell you what happened again. I know you didn't believe me last time, and I don't expect you will believe me now...not until you experience it. Call them when you're ready."

Staring down at the odd message with fascination, I flung my feet over the edge of the couch, suddenly needing a large gulp of tea. Bri's statement was written as if she knew that I would want to leave here one day, that I would want to leave Brian. There was no *if* in her hastily scribbled message. Not only that, it suddenly seemed to me that perhaps she didn't intentionally lie about time traveling back to the seventeenth century. Bri actually believed she'd done just that.

Which changed things and made me worry for her all the more. Even after I found Bri and she told me the elaborate tale, even after I met Blaire, the woman who so closely resembled her that I was certain they had to be related in some manner, I still could not believe my friend's story. There was a reason she felt the need to lie. Frankly, I was so glad to know that Bri was alive and not murdered, buried in a ditch in the middle of Scotland, that I had decided to let it go. Begrudgingly, I'd accepted the fact that I might never know the truth of what happened to her after she disappeared. But if Bri truly believed that she'd traveled back in time, then something terrible must've happened to her.

Her brain was addled, disturbed, and I owed it to her to find out just what and who had done this to her. Not that I didn't need to get away from this place for personal reasons – I certainly did. But a trip to Scotland to find Bri and try to talk her out of her delusions would be the perfect excuse to leave. Better to help someone else out of a problem than to wade in the self-pity I felt at my own.

Making my way back to the front doorway, I found my duffle bag and withdrew my wallet and cell phone. I recalled writing down the phone number for the strange innkeepers I met the last time I searched for Bri. The old couple had been nearly impossible to reach, and I was not altogether sure that I'd be able to make contact with them again. I got the impression that their phone number and address were not readily available.

Finding the slip of paper in my wallet, I clicked the call button on my phone and punched in the number as quickly as I could, not waiting a moment so that I could change my mind. The phone rang once and then was answered by the unmistakable voice of the innkeeper herself.

"Why, Mitsy, how are ye, dear? Jerry and I have been expecting a call from ye any minute. I suggest that ye start packing up yer things, though ye willna need much once ye get here."

My mouth hung open. How did she know it was me who'd called? I doubted that she had caller ID at the little inn. How did she know that I planned on coming there? I'd yet to say a word to her, and I didn't know what to say now. "Um…hi. Why would you expect a call from me?"

The old woman at the other end of the phone laughed softly. "Well, dear, I know a large number of things that I doubt ye would expect me to. Best ye get yerself here and then I will tell ye more. I'm sure ye willna believe a bit of it, though, until ye see it for yerself."

She was certainly right about that. "Ok…uh, is Bri there? May I speak to her for a moment?"

I knew she would tell me Bri wasn't there, but obviously she was. How else would the woman have known that Bri suggested I come there?

"Ye know that she isna here, love. She's a far time away from here to be sure, but ye will see her soon enough. She told me to tell ye when ye called that she doesna wish for ye to pay for yer plane ticket on yer own. She knows your budget is limited. I've already called the airline and purchased a ticket for ye. Yer flight is at 3:00 p.m. tomorrow. All ye need to do is check in at the counter. Yer rental car has been arranged, as well. I suppose since ye found yer way to our inn once before, ye are capable of doing so again. We will see ye soon. Safe travels, Mitsy."

She hung up the phone, and I stared at the wall in confusion. Thank God it was summer. As long as I didn't stay gone for more than a month, I wouldn't have to make arrangements at work.

It seemed that by this time tomorrow, I would find myself on a flight headed to Scotland.

———

Get *Morna's Magic* - **Book 3** to continue reading the rest of the story.

Morna's Magic
(The Magical Matchmaker's Legacy - Book 3)

And don't miss the Christmas Novella:

The Conall's Magical Yuletide
(The Magical Matchmaker's Legacy - Book 2.5)

A Sweet, Scottish,
Time-Travel Romance

USA TODAY BESTSELLING AUTHOR

BETHANY CLAIRE

CONALL'S
MAGICAL
YULETIDE

A NOVELLA

The Magical
Matchmaker's Legacy
BOOK 2.5

LETTER TO READERS

Dear Reader,

I hope you enjoyed *Morna's Secret* (*The Magical Matchmaker's Legacy - Book 2*). Arran and Blaire had to have their chance to make their love story work, so continuing the series was not an option for me.

As an author, I love feedback from readers. You are the reason that I write, and I love hearing from you. If you would like to connect, there are several ways you can do so. You can reach out to me on Facebook or on Twitter or visit my Pinterest boards. If you want to read excerpts from my books, listen to audiobook samples, learn more about me, and find some cool downloadable files related to the books, visit my website.

The best way to stay in touch is to subscribe to my newsletter. Go to my website and subscribe in the box in the middle of the page under "Newsletter" that asks for your email address or submit your email address. If you don't hear from me regularly, please check your spam folder or junk mail to make sure my messages aren't ending up there. Please set up your email to allow my messages through to you so you never miss a new book, a chance to win great prizes or a possible appearance in your area.

Finally, if you enjoyed this book, I would appreciate it so much if you would recommend it to your friends and family. And if you would please take time to review it on Goodreads and/or your favorite retailer site, it would be a great help. Reviews can be tough to come by these days, and you, the reader, have the power to make or break a book.

Thank you so much for reading *Morna's Secret*. I hope you choose to journey with me through the other books in the series.

All my best,
    Bethany

ABOUT THE AUTHOR

BETHANY CLAIRE is a USA Today bestselling author of swoon-worthy, Scottish romance and time travel novels. Bethany loves to immerse her readers in worlds filled with lush landscapes, hunky Scots, lots of magic, and happy endings.

She has two ornery fur-babies, plays the piano every day, and loves Disney and yoga pants more than any twenty-something really should. She is most creative after a good night's sleep and the perfect cup of tea. When not writing, Bethany travels as much as she possibly can, and she never leaves home without a good book to keep her company.

In addition to writing, Bethany is also a sought after self-publishing instructor and advisor who has helped many writers develop a road map to help them succeed in Indie publishing. She is the co-founder of www.masteringselfpublishing.com, a site dedicated to helping Indies create thriving publishing businesses by offering educational resources through online courses and consultations.

If you want to read more about Bethany or if you're curious about when her next book will come out, please visit her website at: www.bethanyclaire.com, where you can sign up to receive email notifications about new releases.

Connect with Bethany on social media, visit her website for lots of book extras, or email her:

www.bethanyclaire.com
bclaire@bethanyclaire.com

ACKNOWLEDGMENTS

Morna's Secret was a difficult book to make "sweet." The storyline between the two main characters is rather adult in nature and the story takes some dark turns in several places. That being said, I think J.J. Archer did a fantastic job helping me change things up enough so the story didn't cross any huge lines. Thank you.

In addition, I would like to thank my proofreading team: Karen Corboy, Elizabeth Halliday, and Johnetta Ivey, thank you so much for your willingness to read these stories. I appreciate your help so much.

Mom, you know that I can never thank you enough for all that you do for me and the business, but I'll do my best to try. ;) Thanks for all you do—you're the best.